THE
CODEBREAKER
KIDS

Other Avon Camelot Books by
George Edward Stanley

THE ITALIAN SPAGHETTI MYSTERY
THE UKRAINIAN EGG MYSTERY

GEORGE EDWARD STANLEY is a professor of Spanish, Italian, and Romanian at Cameron University. He is a past member of the Board of Directors of the Society of Children's Book Writers and is Secretary of the Juvenile Selection Committee of the Mystery Writers of America.

Dr. Stanley now lives in Lawton, Oklahoma, with his wife and two sons.

THE
CODEBREAKER
KIDS

George Edward Stanley

AN AVON  CAMELOT BOOK

THE CODEBREAKER KIDS is an original publication of Avon Books. This work has never before appeared in book form.

AVON BOOKS
A division of
The Hearst Corporation
105 Madison Avenue
New York, New York 10016

Library of Congress Cataloging in Publication Data:

Stanley, George Edward.
  The codebreaker kids.

  (An Avon Camelot book)
  Summary: Three friends form a codebreaking service and meet a motley cast of characters, including a Bulgarian spy, a man from the State Department, and a little old lady who wants her diary encoded.
  [1. Ciphers—Fiction] I. Title.
PZ7.S78694Co   1987   [Fic]   86-26581

First Camelot Printing: May 1987

Chapter One

"Well, they've caught another one!" Mr. Lakewood said. He slammed the newspaper down on the kitchen table.

Mrs. Lakewood put a piece of buttered toast on Mr. Lakewood's plate. "Another what, dear?" she asked.

"Another spy!" Mr. Lakewood bellowed. "What else do they have in Washington to catch?"

Dinky Lakewood's ears perked up. He stopped drinking his orange juice and listened. He was very interested in spies.

"Please don't bellow, Henry," Mrs. Lakewood said. "It's bad for your digestive system."

"Well, it makes me mad," Mr. Lakewood continued, "all these people coming over here to spy on us. And after all the things we've done for them, too! It's un–American, that's what it is!"

"You know, Dad," said Dinky, "I think I'd like to meet a real live spy one of these days."

"Dinky Lakewood!" Mr. Lakewood shouted. "If I ever catch you messing around with a spy, I'll, I'll . . . well, I'll . . . Did you know that the FBI would lock you up and throw away the key?" Mr. Lakewood looked helplessly at his wife. "See, Margaret, see! It's come to

1

this already. We're probably too late. I'm going to move us to Iowa, or even to Kansas!"

Dinky knew that his father would probably never move, but the thought of it bothered him. He didn't want to leave Washington. It was an exciting town. He enjoyed everything about Washington—especially the spies.

"How did the spy get caught, Dad?" Dinky asked.

"Here, you read about it," Mr. Lakewood said. He handed the paper to Dinky. "I'm late for work." Then he gulped down the rest of his coffee.

"Now, Henry, please don't gulp," Mrs. Lakewood said. "You know it's bad for your digestive system."

Mr. Lakewood stood up. "I'll be in around noon," he said. "And, Dinky, I want you to stay out of trouble."

"Okay, Dad," Dinky said. He watched as his father went out the kitchen door and got into his van. The van said LAKEWOOD PLUMBING SUPPLIES on the side. That van would make a good spy van, Dinky thought, although he wasn't quite sure what a good spy van would contain.

Dinky excused himself and took the newspaper up to his room. He lay down on his bed and started reading the article about the spy. He was almost to the end when something the spy said caught his attention:

"I would never have been caught," the spy had told the newspaper reporter, "if I had been working with competent cryptologists. They sent me secret messages that were either too easy or too hard to decode. The trouble with the spy business today is that there isn't anybody in it who's really good at encoding or decoding secret messages."

Dinky felt chills run up and down his spine. It was fate, he thought, seeing this newspaper article at this time.

Last week, on his tenth birthday, his parents had

2

finally given him what he had always wanted: *The Complete and Total Book of All the Secret Codes That Have Ever Been Devised and That Ever Will Be Devised.* Dinky had spent all of his time reading it. And he had solved all of the problem codes at the back of the book—without any problem.

His mind reeled. Would it be possible? he wondered.

He went out into the hall and picked up the telephone. He dialed.

"Hello," a sleepy voice said.

"Wong!" Dinky said. "The clubhouse in ten minutes!" Then he hung up.

He started to dial again. Then he hesitated. But finally he dialed.

"Hello . . . hello . . . hello!" the voice on the line said.

"Lulu . . . (gulp) . . . the clubhouse . . . (gulp) . . . in ten minutes," Dinky managed to say. Then he hung up quickly.

There, he thought, he had done it.

Wong was okay. No problem. He and Dinky had been friends for years. But Lulu Hawthorne? That *was* a problem. Wong might rebel. Lulu was weird. Strange. Crazy, even. But Dinky and Lulu shared one passion: spies. Lulu Hawthorne wanted to be a spy. If there was anybody at Whittier Elementary School who knew more about spies than Dinky Lakewood, it was Lulu Hawthorne. Yes, Lulu had to be a part of this plan, Dinky decided, and Wong would just have to live with it.

From the garage, Dinky got a small board, a small can of black paint, and a small paintbrush. These he carried to the clubhouse at the rear of the Lakewoods' backyard.

The clubhouse had once been a storage shed until Mrs. Lakewood convinced Mr. Lakewood that since the neighborhood kids were going to play in there anyway, he might as well give in and let them have it. Afterwards, there was a noticeable decrease in Mr. Lakewood's blood pressure.

Dinky had just finished painting the word SECRET on the board when Wong arrived.

"What's all the excitement about?" Wong said. "Did the school burn down?"

"Of course not," Dinky said. "You'd have heard the sirens."

"Well what, then?" Wong repeated.

"I want to wait until . . . uh, uh, Lulu is . . . uh, uh . . . here to explain," Dinky said.

"Who did you say? Lulu? Lulu *Hawthorne?* I can't believe what I'm hearing! You mean you've invited that weird Lulu Hawthorne over here?"

"She's necessary to my plan," Dinky said.

"What plan?" Wong asked. "Are you opening up a freak show? Do you need somebody to model Halloween masks for you?"

"Calm down, Wong," Dinky said. "Lulu's not half bad . . . if you just get to know her."

"Well, I guess I'll never know, Dinky Lakewood," Wong shouted, "because I'm leaving!"

Just then the door of the clubhouse opened. Dinky and Wong looked up.

There stood Lulu Hawthorne. She had on a blue beret. Dark glasses covered her eyes. "Why am I here?" she asked, using a foreign accent.

"That's a very good question," Wong said. "I've been trying to find out the answer myself."

"Come in, Lulu," Dinky said, "and have a seat." He moved a chair out for her. She sat down. "I want both of you to forget the past," he continued. "We are about to begin a project which, if it succeeds, will make us—"

"Cut the rhetoric," Lulu said. She was very proud of

4

her vocabulary. "And get to the point!" She stood up and began pacing back and forth.

"Sit down, Lulu," Wong said. "You're making me nervous."

Lulu stopped pacing. She stared at Wong until she finally stared him down. Satisfied, she took a seat at the back of the clubhouse.

"Now, then," Dinky began. He was sweating. There was actually electricity in the air because of the tension. He could feel it. His pants were clinging to his socks. "Now, then," he began again. "I called you here for a very important reason."

"It had better be important," Wong mumbled.

Lulu blew her nose.

"This is an organizational meeting for the Secret Code Service," Dinky continued. He hesitated. Nobody said anything. He relaxed. He took out his handkerchief and wiped the sweat off his forehead. "Our business will be to encode and decode secret messages for spies."

"What spies?" Lulu asked.

"Any spy who comes to us," Dinky said.

"You mean *foreign* spies?" Wong said.

"Well, naturally, we'll have to screen our clients to make sure we aren't breaking any laws by helping them," Dinky said.

"Do you think we'll get much business?" Wong asked. "Personally, I don't know a thing about secret codes."

Lulu snorted. "You guys are such amateurs," she said. "I'm leaving."

"Wait a minute," Dinky shouted. "Let me read you something from this morning's newspaper." He unfolded the newspaper and read the article about the spy.

"Do you really think we could make a fortune?" Wong asked. "I sure could use a new bike."

"I think there's a definite possibility," Dinky said.

Lulu stood up. "Wait a minute, wait a minute," she said. "I know you're pretty good at encoding and decoding secret messages, Dinky Lakewood, but you're talking about the big time now. The only reason you won the Whittier Elementary School Secret Message Decoding Competition was because I didn't enter. This is going to be different. Are you ready? Are you up to it?"

"I'm ready," Dinky said. He paused. "At least I think I am. I *did* solve all the problem codes in the back of *The Complete and Total Book of All the Secret Codes That Have Ever Been Devised and That Ever Will Be Devised.*"

"When did you do that?" Lulu asked.

"Last week," Dinky said.

Lulu took off her dark glasses. "I'm impressed," she said.

Dinky felt himself swelling with pride. Lulu Hawthorne didn't pass out compliments frequently.

"How'll all these spies know we're going to do this?" Wong asked.

Dinky hadn't considered that. He thought for a minute. Finally, he said, "We'll advertise, just like everybody else does."

"In the *Washington Post?*" Wong said.

"We can't afford the *Washington Post,*" Lulu said. "Advertising costs a lot of money."

"What, then?" Wong asked.

Dinky took out a piece of paper. "I had something like this in mind," he said. He started printing:

ATTENTION ALL SPIES

If you're having trouble understanding
your secret messages, bring them to us
for decoding. You can trust us. Our
motto is: YOUR SECRETS ARE OUR SECRETS!

SECRET CODE SERVICE
4532 Ross Avenue, Rear
Washington, D.C.   Tel. No.: 555-3429

Dinky Lakewood, Head Cryptologist

Lulu looked at the piece of paper. "Who appointed you Head Cryptologist?" she demanded.

Dinky began to think that Wong had been right. Lulu was going to be a very difficult person to work with. He decided that it was time to take a stand. "I did!" he announced.

Lulu stiffened but said nothing. She looked back down at the advertisement. "Well, that's fine for decoding," she said finally, "but what about the encoding you mentioned earlier? What about all those spies out there who are having trouble putting their messages into secret code? What are you going to offer *them*?"

"We'll solve that problem," Dinky said. He started printing at the bottom of the piece of paper:

Or if you have a message you want
written in code, then the Secret
Code Service can do that, too.
YOUR ENEMIES WILL NEVER FIGURE IT
OUT!

Lulu picked up the advertisement and looked at it again. "Not bad," she said, "not bad."

"But what are we going to do with it?" Wong asked.

"Do you think your dad might let us make copies of it on his duplicating machine?" Dinky said.

"I guess he wouldn't mind," Wong said.

"Then we can simply deliver the copies door to door," Dinky added.

"Hold it!" Lulu said. "This spy does not go from door to door. Besides, that would never work. We'd have to have too many copies. I have a better idea."

7

"Well, let's hear it," Dinky said.

"After Wong duplicates the advertisement, he can give the copies to me," Lulu explained, "and then I can ride all over Washington on the Metrobuses and leave the advertisements in the seats. I'm quite sure that spies ride buses. I'm positive that I've seen them before."

"That's an excellent idea," Dinky said. He was certain that if anybody could recognize a spy, it was Lulu Hawthorne.

"Well, then, let's get started," Lulu said.

Dinky wasn't quite sure he liked the way Lulu had suddenly taken over, but he decided not to press the issue this time. "Wong, you take the advertisement to your father's office and duplicate it," he said. "Make as many copies as he'll let you make. Then you can take the copies to Lulu's house so she can start riding the buses this afternoon."

"Okay," Wong said.

"Agreed," Lulu said. "And we'll all meet back here tomorrow afternoon for progress reports."

"Good," Dinky said. "Then I now declare the Secret Code Service officially in business!"

Chapter Two

Dinky had just finished painting the sign that said SECRET CODE SERVICE and had nailed it to the front of the clubhouse when Wong and Lulu arrived the next afternoon.

"Looks nice," Wong said.

"If somewhat unprofessional," Lulu added.

"It'll do," Dinky said, "until we can afford to have a real one made. Come on in. Let's have the progress reports."

The three of them went inside the clubhouse. Dinky took his place in front. Wong sat down in an armchair. Lulu sat down on a bench in the back.

"You first, Wong," Dinky said.

Wong stood up. "Well, I took the advertisement to my dad's office, and I asked his secretary to make one hundred copies of it," he began. "She only made twenty-five, because the machine broke down. Boy, was my dad ever mad about that!"

"Twenty-five's not very many," Dinky said.

"Well, I couldn't help it," Wong insisted.

"Okay, go on," Dinky coaxed.

"That's it," Wong said. "I took the twenty-five copies over to Lulu's house and gave them to her."

"All right, Lulu," Dinky said, "let's have your report."

9

Lulu stood up. She took off her beret and placed it neatly on the bench. Then she took off her dark glasses, folded them, and placed them on top of the beret. "Of course you must realize that I was working under a handicap," she began.

"What do you mean?" Dinky asked.

"Having only twenty-five copies of the advertisement to work with," Lulu continued, "I had to be very selective about which buses I rode."

"We appreciate your selectivity," Dinky said. "Please continue with your report."

"I took the twenty-five copies that Wong gave me and rode *selected* Metrobuses all over the District and into Maryland and Virginia," Lulu said. "I left one copy on each bus I rode. I am quite positive that there were spies on several of the buses."

"That's excellent, men . . . uh, gang," Dinky said.

"Oh, yes, this is for you," Lulu added. She handed Dinky a piece of paper.

"What's this?" Dinky asked.

"It's my expense account," Lulu said.

"Your *what?*" Wong said.

"That piece of paper shows how much it cost me to ride all those buses," Lulu said.

"I can't pay for this!" Dinky cried.

"I expect to be reimbursed," Lulu insisted.

"Well, can't you wait?" Dinky said.

"For what?" Lulu demanded.

"Well . . . until we get our first customer, that's what!" Dinky said.

Lulu thought for a minute. "All right," she said finally. "But I won't forget this!"

Dinky was sure she wouldn't.

"Oh, Mr. Lakewood!" There was a knock at the clubhouse door. "Mr. Lakewood!"

"Quiet!" Lulu whispered. She put a finger to her

10

lips. "It could be danger!" She hurriedly put on her dark glasses and her beret.

The knocking continued. "Oh, Mr. Lakewood!"

Dinky looked at Lulu. "I think we should open the door," he whispered.

Lulu thought for a minute. "Okay," she said, "but do it slowly."

Dinky slowly opened the door.

A little old lady with white hair was standing outside. She was leaning on a cane. "Is there a Mr. Lakewood in there?" she asked.

"I'm Mr. . . . uh, I'm Dinky Lakewood," Dinky said.

"May I come in?" the little old lady asked.

"Yes, of course," Dinky said. "Here, take this chair."

"Thank you very much," the little old lady said. It took her a few minutes to sit down.

"Now, then, what can we do for you?" Dinky asked.

"I'm Emma Temple," the little old lady said. "You may call me Emma. I've come about your advertisement." Emma opened her purse and took out a piece of paper. "I found this on my bus yesterday, and I'm interested in your services."

"It worked!" Wong shouted.

Lulu beamed proudly at a job well done.

"Are you a spy?" Dinky asked.

"Oh, good heavens, no," Emma said, "but I do need something written in a secret code."

"Well, Emma, we were really expecting a spy," Lulu said. "We cater mostly to spies. I'm sorry." She took off her beret and dark glasses.

"Oh dear, and I was so in hopes that you could help me," Emma said. She sounded very disappointed. She stood up. "Well, thank you very much."

"Just a minute," Dinky said. "Let me think. We might be able to help you."

"Dinky Lakewood!" Lulu protested.

Dinky raised his hand for silence. "But you'll have to remember that this is a business," he continued, "and we charge for our services."

"That's all right," Emma said.

"I'm talking about *money*," Dinky said.

"I am, too," Emma retorted.

"Okay," Dinky said, "but first you need to fill out a card for our files."

"All right," Emma said.

Dinky handed her a three-by-five index card. "Just write your name, address, telephone number, and occupation," he said.

"My, my," Emma exclaimed, "this is such an efficient organization. I'm impressed."

Lulu snorted.

Dinky gave her a dirty look. "Okay," he said, retrieving the card from Emma, "that's fine, just fine. Here, Mr. Chiang, will you please put this card in our file?" He held the card out to Wong.

"What do you want me to do with it?" Wong said.

Dinky flushed. "Just take it," he said through clenched teeth. He turned back to Emma. "Now, what was it that you wanted to put into secret code?" he asked.

"My diary," Emma said. "My younger sister Ethel keeps reading it. I've hidden it all over our house, and she is still able to find it. Nothing I can do will convince her not to read my diary. You know how this younger generation is!"

"I think that's terrible," Wong said.

"She's unscrupulous," Emma asserted.

"How old is she?" Lulu asked.

"She's seventy-five," Emma said, "but she tells everybody that she's seventy-four. She is totally without morals!"

"May I look at your diary?" Dinky asked.

12

Emma hesitated. "Well, I guess you'll have to see it in order to put it into code, won't you?"

"That's usually the way it works," Dinky said, trying to be polite.

Emma handed Dinky the diary, and he began reading to himself: *"I watched another episode of 'The Stormy Secret' today and fell in love with Dr. Beach."*

"You can see that it's very steamy stuff," Emma said. "It's embarrassing to have Ethel read it. She teases me in front of Mother."

Dinky nodded. "I can see why you would want this in secret code, all right," he said.

"How much do you charge?" Emma asked.

"Well, we haven't figured out our rate schedule for diaries yet," Dinky said, "but—"

"I'll pay you five dollars a page," Emma interrupted, "and no more!"

"I was going to say that five dollars a page would sound about right," Dinky continued.

Lulu opened her mouth. "We're going to be rich!" she gasped.

"I know exactly which bike I'm going to buy," Wong declared.

"Now there are two ways of having your diary entries encoded," Dinky explained. "We can teach you how to put them into code, or each day you can bring us what you've written and we can encode it for you."

"Why don't you teach me how to do it?" Emma said. "That sounds exciting."

"We also charge five dollars for lessons," Lulu said.

"I'm good for it," Emma said.

"All right," Dinky said. He sat down beside Emma. "Why don't we start out with what is called an inverse alphabet?"

"You'll have to explain that," Emma said.

Wong and Lulu crowded around to watch.

"Here, look at this," Dinky began. He took a pencil and a piece of paper. "We'll write out the regular Latin alphabet here—this is also called the *clear alphabet*— and then, under it, we'll write the same alphabet backwards.":

A B C D E F G H I J K L M N O P Q R S T U V W X Y Z
Z Y X W V U T S R Q P O N M L K J I H G F E D C B A

"Now what do I do?" Emma asked.

"Well, you first write out what you want to enter in your diary," Dinky said. "This is called the *clear message*. Then you encode it by using the inverse alphabet. Let's do the first four words of the entry you showed me: 'I WATCHED ANOTHER EPISODE.' Now find the letter 'I' in the top alphabet and look at the letter *underneath* it in the inverse alphabet."

"It's 'R,' " Emma said.

"Right," Dinky said. "And every time you have the letter 'I' in your clear message, you'll write the letter 'R' in code."

"I see," Emma said.

"That's neat," Wong said.

Lulu smiled a knowing smile.

"Now, then," Dinky said, "let's do the rest of the words. You want to try, Emma?"

"Okay," Emma said. "I think I can do it. For 'WATCHED,' 'W' is 'D,' 'A' is 'Z,' 'T' is 'G,' 'C' is 'X,' 'H' is 'S,' 'E' is 'V,' and 'D' is 'W,' so 'WATCHED' in code is 'DZGXSVW,' and 'I WATCHED' is 'R DZGXSVW.' Oh, Mr. Lakewood, how can I ever thank you?"

Dinky smiled. "Well, while you're here, why don't you encode the whole entry," he said, "then I can check it to make sure it's correct before you leave?"

"That's a good idea," Emma said.

Emma worked steadily for several minutes. Wong watched in amazement. Lulu continued to smile her knowing smile. Dinky stood around looking pleased with himself.

Finally, Emma finished encoding the entry. It read: R DZGXSVW ZMLGSVI VKRHLWV LU GSV HGLINB HVXIVG GLWZB ZMW UVOO RM OLEV DRGS WI YVZXS.

"Excellent!" Dinky said.

Wong and Lulu applauded.

"Ethel will never figure this out!" Emma shouted.

"If you really want to make it difficult to decode," Dinky said, "then instead of leaving spaces between the words, write all the letters together like this": RDZGXS-VWZMLGSVIVKRHLWVLUGSVHGLINBHVXIVGG-LWZBZMWUVOORMOLEVDRGSWIYVZXS.

"What if I forget what it says?" Emma said. "What if I want to go back someday and . . . and remember? What do I do then?"

"Then you decode it by doing the reverse of what you just did," Dinky said. "Take each letter in the coded message and look at the alphabet letter *above* it. If you wrote all the letters together when you encoded the message, then the clear message would come out looking like this": IWATCHEDANOTHEREPISODE-OFTHESTORMYSECRETTODAYANDFELLINLOVE-WITHDRBEACH." But you'd be able to separate the words once you had decoded the message."

"That's brilliant," Emma said. "Oh, Mr. Lakewood, Mr. Lakewood, how can I ever thank you? Now I can express all my innermost feelings and Ethel won't know what I'm saying."

"That's what we're here for," Dinky said.

"Well, here's ten dollars," Emma said. "It's worth every penny. Oh, I just feel so good!"

Lulu took the two five-dollar bills from Dinky

and held them up to the light. "They're real!" she said.

Wong gasped.

"Thank you very much, Emma," Dinky said. "We really appreciate your business."

After Emma had left, Dinky said, "I guess we ought to open up a bank account to handle all this money."

"Don't forget the money you owe me for bus fares yesterday," Lulu said.

"Oh, okay," Dinky said. He paused. "Did you save your receipts?"

"What receipts?" Lulu asked.

"Didn't you ask for receipts from the bus drivers to prove that you actually rode those buses?" Dinky asked.

"Well, no, I . . . I . . ." Lulu stammered.

"Well, that's all right this time," Dinky said, "but from now on, we're going to do this right! Receipts have to be presented with expense accounts before anybody gets paid. This is a real business!"

Lulu looked chastised.

"Dinky! Telephone!"

"That's my mom," Dinky said. "I'll be right back. You guys start thinking about what we're going to do with all the money we're going to make."

"In a way, I'm disappointed," Lulu said.

Dinky stopped at the door. "Why?" he asked.

"Yeah, why?" Wong repeated.

"Well, I thought our first customer would be a real spy," Lulu complained. "Instead, we get a little old lady and her diary."

"Don't be unkind, Lulu," Dinky said. "You'll be old one of these days, too. Besides, we made ten dollars, didn't we?"

"Yeah," Wong said, "give us time. After all, we just sent out the advertisements yesterday. I think that's pretty good. At least we know that *somebody* saw them."

"Dinky!" Mrs. Lakewood shouted again. "Telephone!"

"Coming, Mom!" Dinky cried. "I'll be right back," he said to Lulu and Wong.

Dinky went into the kitchen. "Who is it, Mom?" he asked.

"It's a man's voice," Mrs. Lakewood said. "I didn't recognize it. He wants to speak to a Mr. Dinky Lakewood of the Secret Code Service. What are you up to, son?"

"Nothing, Mom," Dinky said, picking up the receiver. "Just having fun, that's all. Hello!"

"Is this Mr. Lakewood?" the voice on the phone said.

"Yes, yes, it is," Dinky said.

There was a pause on the line, then the voice said, "You are *the* Mr. Dinky Lakewood of the Secret Code Service?"

"Yes, I am Mr. . . . uh, I mean, yes, this is Dinky Lakewood," Dinky said. "What can I do for you?"

"Is it true what you said on that piece of paper I found on the bus yesterday?" the voice asked.

"Oh, that. Yes, yes, it is," Dinky answered. His heart was pounding. "Do you have some work for us?"

"I might," the voice replied.

"Well, we're really experts," Dinky claimed.

"You're not with the CIA, are you?" the voice asked.

"No," Dinky said, "we're not."

"Or DI6 or the FBI or—"

"We're totally independent of any government," Dinky interrupted. "Our motto is: 'Your Secrets Are Our Secrets!' " Dinky noticed that his mother was staring at him. He turned towards the wall.

"You're not Chinese?" the voice demanded.

Dinky hesitated. "No, *I'm* not," he said.

"Then I'll be at your office in fifteen minutes," the voice said. "First, I have to make sure that I'm not being followed."

"All right. I understand," Dinky said. "But . . . how will I recognize you?"

"What do you mean?" the voice said.

"I mean, when you come, how will I know it's you and not somebody pretending to be you?" Dinky said.

"You have a point there," the voice said. "Let me think. Oh, yes, I have a very red nose today."

"What?" Dinky said. "Hello . . . hello . . . hello!" He hung up the receiver.

"Who was that?" Mrs. Lakewood asked.

"Just a customer," Dinky replied.

"A *what?*" Mrs. Lakewood asked in vain, for Dinky was already out the kitchen door and rushing back to the clubhouse with the news.

"Listen, gang," he said, "we're going to have our first *real* customer!"

"Emma was pretty real, if you ask me," Wong said. He was looking at the two five-dollar bills.

"Do you mean what I think you mean?" Lulu asked.

"I do," Dinky replied.

Lulu picked up her beret and dark glasses and put them on. "I'm ready," she said.

"Oh, I get it," Wong said slowly. "This time it's a *real* spy!"

"You've never met a more real spy in your life," Dinky declared. "He knows just what to say."

"I've never met a spy before, period!" Wong said.

"I wonder what he'll look like," Lulu said.

"That's the strange part," Dinky said.

"What do you mean, 'strange'?" Lulu asked.

"He said he had a red nose today," Dinky replied.

Chapter Three

"He'd better hurry up and get here," Wong said. "I have to go home soon. I need to do my English homework."

Dinky frowned. "Oh, I'd forgotten about that," he said. "We're having a test tomorrow, aren't we?"

Wong nodded.

"It sure is dark in here," Lulu said. "How late is it?"

"Well, it's late," Dinky said, "but it's not *that* late. Why don't you take off those dark glasses?"

"Oh," Lulu said. She took off the glasses.

There was a sudden noise outside the clubhouse door. Everyone looked up, startled. Lulu hurriedly put her dark glasses back on.

The door began to open slowly. A tall man stood silhouetted in the doorway. A fedora was pulled down over his eyes. But Dinky would have recognized him anywhere. He had a very red nose.

"I'm looking for a Mr. Lakewood," the man said. "Is he here?"

Wong pointed a trembling finger at Dinky.

"I'm Dinky Lakewood," Dinky said. "Come in."

The man looked at Wong, then at Dinky. "Are you sure you people don't work for the Chinese?" he asked.

"No, no, I'm positive," Dinky assured him. "We're completely independent."

The man came inside the clubhouse. He sat down in a vacant chair. "This is a nice setup you have here," he said. "Nobody would believe this!"

"Thanks," Dinky said, "but we're just getting started. We hope to get some better equipment soon, like new chairs and tables, and maybe even a telephone."

"Yeah, this is real nice," the man said, looking around.

"Was there something that we could help you with?" Dinky finally asked. He could feel his voice trembling.

The man looked first at Dinky, then at Wong and Lulu. "How do you know that I am who you think I am?" he asked.

Dinky pointed an unsteady finger at the man's nose. "You said you'd have a red nose," he said, "and you certainly have a very red nose."

"Oh, yes, that," the man acknowledged. "My nose is very sensitive to the sun. Strange, but that's the only place I get a sunburn."

"That is strange," Dinky said. Wong and Lulu nodded. "Now, then, was there something—"

"Yes," the man interrupted. "I'm having trouble figuring out this secret message from my government." He handed Dinky a piece of paper. "I'm sure it's important."

Dinky studied the message for a moment. "I'll need to look at your codebook," he said. "You do have a codebook, don't you?"

"Oh, yes, I've got one just like all the rest of us spies," the man said. He felt in his coat pocket and took out a small black book. "Here it is." He handed it to Dinky. "It certainly hasn't been much help to me, though."

"Well, that's what *we're* here for," Dinky said. He

looked at the book. In red letters on the front, it said: *All the Bulgarian Codes You'll Ever Need!* He flipped through the pages. Then he looked again at the coded message the man had given him. "Hmm. Yes, I think we'll be able to help you. But I'm curious. Weren't you trained to do this yourself?"

The man's face turned as red as his nose. He lowered his eyes. "I have a confession to make," he said. "I cheated all the way through Sofia Spy School. The girl across the aisle from me let me copy off her papers. I was young and innocent and . . ."

Dinky held up his hand for silence. "You needn't explain," he said. "We here at the Secret Code Service do not pass judgment on our customers!"

The man looked up. "Oh, thank you, thank you," he said, "thank you so very much!"

"It's nothing," Dinky said. He began to relax. "Before we begin, we need to fill out a card on you for our files."

"Oh, well now, I don't know about that," the man protested.

Dinky raised his hand again. "It's perfectly all right," he said. "We do this for all our customers. Nobody has access to these cards but the members of the Secret Code Service."

"Well, if you're sure you're the only ones," the man said.

"Mr. Chiang, will you make a card for this gentleman?" Dinky said.

"Certainly," Wong said. He got a three-by-five index card and a pencil. "Name?"

"Boris Bulgar," the man replied.

"Address?" Wong continued.

"1601 Pennsylvania Avenue," Boris said.

"Telephone number?" Wong said.

"555-5555," Boris replied.

"Let's see," Wong said. "I'll just put your occupation down as 'spy'; is that all right?"

"That's correct," Boris said.

"Okay, that's it, Mr. Lakewood," Wong said, handing the card to Dinky.

"Thank you, Mr. Chiang," Dinky said. "Now, then, Mr. Bulgar—"

"Please, just call me Boris," Boris interrupted.

"All right, Boris," Dinky said, "I have looked at this coded message, and I think we'll be able to help you."

"How much do you charge?" Boris asked.

"Well, we've not established our rates for secret documents yet," Dinky said, "but—"

"I'll pay you five a page and no more," Boris said.

"I think that five dollars a page would be sufficient," Dinky continued.

"Five *dollars!*" Boris exclaimed. "Who's talking about dollars? I was talking about *leva.*"

"What's a *leva?*" Wong asked.

"A *lev* is the currency of my country," Boris said. "I'm afraid it's all I have. I need my dollars to live on!"

"Well, I'm sure that our International Banking Department can take care of you when the time comes to make payment," Dinky said. He nodded towards Lulu, who was still sitting silently at the back of the clubhouse.

"Good enough," Boris said. "Now what about my secret message?"

"It looks like a variation of the Caesar Code," Dinky said. "That's just a simple substitution code."

Boris looked hurt. "Why did you say 'simple'?" he asked.

"I was only speaking in relative terms, of course," Dinky said hurriedly. "Any code will be difficult if . . . well, what I'm trying to say is—"

22

"Can you figure out what it says?" Boris interrupted.

Lulu had taken off her dark glasses and had moved closer to Boris. "I'm Lulu Hawthorne," she said, sticking out her hand for Boris to shake. Boris looked up, startled. "I'm planning to be a spy, too," Lulu continued. "I'd like to get to know you better. Maybe we could exchange information."

"What's with her?" Boris asked Dinky.

"Lulu knows more about spies than anybody else in Whittier Elementary School," Dinky said.

Lulu beamed proudly.

Boris shook her hand. "Yeah? Well maybe we could get together sometime," he said. "You got any secrets you want to sell?"

"I could probably—" Lulu began.

"Lulu!" Dinky protested. "Remember the integrity of the Secret Code Service!"

Lulu stopped suddenly. She withdrew her hand from Boris's grasp. "Oh, I'm sorry," she said hurriedly. "I don't know what came over me. This is a serious business, Boris. Anything we learn here at the Secret Code Service stays right here. We can't be compromised."

"Okay, okay," Boris said. "I'm sorry I asked."

Dinky exhaled slowly. Our first real test of character, he thought. "Now, then, let's look at this message," he said to Boris. WKH VKLS VDLOV DW GDZQ LQ VWDQWRQ SDUN.

"I just can't make heads or tails out of it," Boris said. "What do you think?"

"Well, the first thing we need to do is run down the alphabet," Dinky said. "We can test the first few letters of the message."

"I'm game," Boris said.

Dinky took out a clean sheet of paper and a pencil. "We'll write out the first few letters of the message at the top of the page like this," he said:

"And then we'll run down the alphabet under each letter. Let me show you." Dinky began writing:

W	K	H		V	K	L	S
X	L	I		W	L	M	T
Y	M	J		X	M	N	U
Z	N	K		Y	N	O	V
A	O	L		Z	O	P	W
B	P	M		A	P	Q	X
C	Q	N		B	Q	R	Y
D	R	O		C	R	S	Z
E	S	P		D	S	T	A
F	T	Q		E	T	U	B
G	U	R		F	U	V	C
H	V	S		G	V	W	D
I	W	T		H	W	X	E
J	X	U		I	X	Y	F
K	Y	V		J	Y	Z	G
L	Z	W		K	Z	A	H
M	A	X		L	A	B	I
N	B	Y		M	B	C	J
O	C	Z		N	C	D	K
P	D	A		O	D	E	L
Q	E	B		P	E	F	M
R	F	C		Q	F	G	N
S	G	D		R	G	H	O
T	H	E		S	H	I	P
U	I	F		T	I	J	Q
V	J	G		U	J	K	R

"Now, let's go down the columns and see if there are any recognizable words."

Dinky used his index finger to guide his eyes down the first column of three letters. Boris, Wong, and Lulu huddled closely around him.

"Look!" Wong shouted. "The third horizontal line from the bottom. There's the word 'THE'!"

"You're right," Lulu said, "and on the same line following the word 'THE' is the word 'SHIP.' "

"THE SHIP!" Boris shouted. "That's wonderful. Let's do the—"

"Oh, Mr. Lakewood!"

Dinky looked up.

"That sounds like Emma," Wong said.

"Who's Emma?" Boris asked. "Is she CIA?"

"Good heavens, no!" Lulu said.

Emma opened the door of the clubhouse and came in.

"What's wrong, Emma?" Dinky said. "We're awfully busy now. What do you need?"

"I either want my ten dollars back," Emma announced, "or I want a new secret code!"

Boris looked at Dinky. "I thought you said she wasn't CIA!" he cried.

"She's not," Dinky said.

"Well, she's talking codes," Boris persisted, "and she looks like a spy I once knew in Berlin."

"Emma, have you ever been to Berlin?" Dinky asked.

"Oh, yes," Emma said, "yes, I have."

"I told you so," Boris said. He scrambled to pick up his papers. "I'm getting out of here!"

"I was there in 1923," Emma continued.

Boris stopped. "In 1923!" he said. "I wasn't even born until 1942."

"That's nice, young man," Emma said.

Boris turned towards Dinky. "She couldn't be the spy I knew," he said.

"I told you so," Dinky said. "Now, Emma, what's wrong?"

"Well, I went home," Emma explained, "and I used the secret code you taught me. Then I showed my diary to Ethel, so she could see that there wouldn't be any sense in her trying to find it anymore, because she wouldn't be able to read it."

"And?" Lulu said.

"She read it!" Emma said. "It took her all of ten seconds to figure out that code! I was humiliated!"

"That's terrible," Wong said.

"That's great," Boris said. "I wonder if she'd be interested in working for me. I sure could use somebody like that."

"She's unscrupulous," Emma said. "So I either want a new code or I want my ten dollars back!"

"We'll figure out a new code for you," Dinky said hurriedly. "But can you wait a few minutes? We have another customer."

"Of course," Emma said. She sat down. "I brought my knitting, so I'll just busy myself with that."

"Is this place always this busy?" Boris asked.

"Not yet," Lulu said, "but we're working on it."

"Now, then," Dinky said, "where were we?"

"You were decoding my secret message," Boris said.

"Oh, yes. Well, by the process of running down the alphabet," Dinky continued, "you can see that we can arrive at how the message was encoded."

"Well, come on," Boris said, "let's run down the alphabet some more!"

"It isn't necessary," Dinky said. "By doing just a few letters of the message, we can see that the code alphabet has been slid to the right twenty-three places under the clear alphabet. All we have to do is write out the clear alphabet and the code alphabet under it and we can finish decoding the message." Dinky started writing:

A B C D E F G H I J K L M N O P Q R S T U V W X Y Z
D E F G H I J K L M N O P Q R S T U V W X Y Z A B C

"Well, how do you know with which letter to start the code alphabet?" Boris asked.

"When we ran down the alphabet," Dinky explained, "we saw that the first letter in the secret message, 'W,' was decoded by the letter 'T,' so we know that 'W' in the code alphabet equals 'T' in the clear alphabet. Under 'T' in the clear alphabet, we write 'W' and continue on down the alphabet until each letter in the clear alphabet has its equivalent in the code alphabet.''

"Oh," Boris said, "that's interesting."

"Now," Dinky said, "for the rest of the message: 'VDLOV' equals 'SAILS,' because as you can see, 'V' equals 'S,' 'D' equals 'A,' 'L' equals 'I,' 'O' equals 'L,' and 'V' equals 'S.' "

"That's really clever," Wong said.

"Yeah," Emma added, "this is getting interesting."

Boris looked up at Emma. "Are you sure you're not a spy?" he said.

"No, but I think my sister Ethel is," Emma said. "And if she keeps this up, I'm going to turn her in!"

Dinky cleared his throat. "I wasn't through," he said.

"Then please continue," Boris said.

" 'DW' equals 'AT,' " Dinky said. " 'GDZQ' equals 'DAWN,' 'LQ' equals 'IN,' 'VWDQWRQ' equals 'STANTON,' and 'SDUN' equals 'PARK.' "

" 'THE SHIP SAILS AT DAWN IN STANTON PARK,' " Lulu said. "What kind of a crazy message is that?"

"We have a very elaborate spy system," Boris said. "Sometimes we have to pick up two messages before we can get one complete message. The main part of this message is 'THE SHIP SAILS AT DAWN.' 'STANTON PARK' tells me where the rest of the message is. We do this in case we're being followed and somebody captures us. Then they'll get only one part of the message."

"That's clever," Wong said.

"Yes, it is," Boris said. "But it's also hard to

remember. Thank goodness it's optional. I seldom use two-part messages myself.''

"But where in Stanton Park?" Lulu asked.

"Our drops are always in hollow trees in the center of a park," Boris said. "I need to go to Stanton Park and get the rest of this message. Will you guys still be here to help me decode it?"

"Sure," Lulu said.

Dinky looked at his watch. "It's getting late," he said, "and I have some homework to do. Do you think it'll take you very long?"

"I need to be going home soon, too," Wong said.

Boris looked crestfallen.

Lulu gave a disgusted sigh. "Go on to Stanton Park and get the message, Boris," she said. "I'll still be here. I've been known to do a little decoding in my day, too." She looked directly at Dinky and Wong. "There's at least *one* professional in this organization!"

Dinky and Wong flushed.

"Stanton Park's not too far from here," Boris said. "I'll take a Metrobus and be there and back in no time." He started towards the clubhouse door. "Oh yeah, I almost forgot. Do you want me to pay now or later?"

"Well, you can pay now for this one," Lulu said, "and then you can pay us later for the message you find in Stanton Park."

"Okay," Boris said, "here're five *leva*." He started for the door again, then stopped and turned. "Thanks, guys," he added, "you've saved my job."

After Boris had left, Dinky said, "You know, I like Boris, but I wonder if we should have taken him on as a client. After all, he *is* an enemy agent."

"What do you mean?" Wong said. "Didn't you *screen* him?"

"Well, uh, sort of," Dinky said. He flushed. "But we may be committing treason by helping him."

"Dinky Lakewood, I'm going to be absolutely furious with you if I get sent to prison because of this," Lulu said.

"I just wish somebody would send Ethel to prison," Emma said. "She's so unscrupulous."

Dinky turned. "Oh, it's you, Emma," he said. "I'm sorry. I had forgotten you were here."

"Do you think you could figure out a new secret code for me now?" Emma said. "I have a lot of things that I want to write in my diary before I get to bed tonight."

Dinky sighed. "Sure, Emma," he said, "let me see your diary." Emma handed him the diary. Dinky flipped through some of the pages. "You mean Ethel actually decoded this all by herself?" he said. "She must be very good at cryptology."

"I think she has a criminal mind," Emma said. "I think she's headed for a life of crime."

"I suppose we could develop a code that uses a key word," Dinky said. "I think that would work."

"What do you mean?" Emma asked.

"Well, first you think of a word," Dinky explained. "Something that you'll remember, maybe something that describes Ethel."

"That's easy," Emma said. "*Unscrupulous!*"

"Okay," Dinky said, "now we'll write that word down at the top of a sheet of paper." Dinky printed in large letters:

U N S C R U P U L O U S

"Then, we'll mark out all of the duplicate letters":

U N S C R U̶ P U̶ L O U̶ S̶

"That leaves us with UNSCRPLO. Now, we add the rest of the alphabet, leaving out all of the letters that have already been used, and we have our code alphabet":

U N S C R P L O A B D E F G H I J K M Q T V W X Y Z

"Above it, we write the clear alphabet, and we're now ready to encode messages." Dinky continued writing:

A B C D E F G H I J K L M N O P Q R S T U V W X Y Z
U N S C R P L O A B D E F G H I J K M Q T V W X Y Z

"How clever," Wong said.

"Incredible," Emma said.

Lulu yawned.

"What was the message you wanted to put in your diary?" Dinky asked.

"Here," Emma said. She blushed as she handed Dinky a sheet of paper.

Dinky read the sentence on the paper: *Today I watched 'Life at the Rest Home' and fell in love with Dr. Bellflower.*

"I couldn't bear to have Ethel find that out," Emma said.

"Well, maybe this code will work," Dinky said. "We'll begin with the word 'TODAY.' Find the letter 'T' in the clear alphabet and look below it."

" 'T' equals 'Q,' " Emma said.

"Correct," Dinky said, "and if we follow through, doing the same thing for the remaining letters, 'TODAY' becomes 'QHCUY.' The complete message would be"—Dinky's mind worked rapidly, like a computer—"would be: QHCUY A WUQSORC EAPR UQ QOR KRMQ OHFR UGC PREE AG EHVR WAQO CK NREEPEHWRK."

"Oh, Mr. Lakewood," Emma cried, "why didn't you let me do the rest of it?"

"Please, Emma, please," Dinky begged. "This has been a very long day."

"Well," Emma said, "are you sure this one will work?"

"Emma, you're never sure of anything in the spy business," Dinky said, "but I certainly hope so. Remember, our work is guaranteed or your money back or a new code."

"Thanks," Emma said. "I can't wait to show this to Ethel. She'll be so mad!"

Emma left the clubhouse and disappeared into the darkness.

"Dinky! Dinky Lakewood!"

"It's Mom," Dinky said. He stuck his head out the door. "What do you want, Mom?"

"I can't hold dinner for you any longer," Mrs. Lakewood shouted. "The football games are finally over, and your father is ready to eat!"

"I can't come in now," Dinky shouted back. "I'm in the middle of a very important meeting."

"All right," Mrs. Lakewood called back, "I'll just put it in the oven."

"I certainly hope that Boris shows up soon," Dinky said to Wong and Lulu, "because I *am* getting awfully hungry."

"I am, too," Wong said, "and I really do need to study for that English test. I flunked the last one. This is my last chance to get a passing grade in the course."

"Food, English tests," Lulu said with a sneer. "You two are so . . . so . . . bourgeois, that's what!"

"Well, we—" Dinky began.

"Shhh!" Lulu whispered. "What was that?"

"I didn't hear anything," Dinky said.

"Me, either," Wong said.

31

"There's somebody out there," Lulu said. "Listen!"

"It's me," Boris said, sticking his head inside the clubhouse door. He grinned. "I bet you didn't even know there was anybody around."

"Well, actually—" Dinky started to say.

"That's because I am a highly trained spy," Boris continued. "I am able to slip up on people without making a sound."

Lulu snorted.

"Did you find the message in Stanton Park?" Dinky asked.

"Yes, I did," Boris said, "and it was just as I suspected. I can't figure this one out, either."

"Let me see it," Dinky said.

Boris handed him the message.

Dinky looked at it closely: WZ VO IZR TJMF CVMWJM VO YVRI VIY OVFZ KDXOPMZN JA OCZ VYHDMVG JCVMV RCZI DO NVDGN. "This shouldn't be too difficult to decode, Boris," he said. "It's another variation of the Caesar Code. All you have to do is run down the alphabet, like I showed you with the last message."

DINKY WILL DECODE THIS MESSAGE AT THE BEGINNING OF THE NEXT CHAPTER. DO YOU THINK YOU CAN DO IT BEFORE HE DOES?

Chapter Four

"Here's the decoded message," Dinky said.

"Let me see," Boris said. " 'BE AT NEW YORK HARBOR AT DAWN AND TAKE PICTURES OF THE ADMIRAL O'HARA WHEN IT SAILS,' " he read. "Gee, how in the world did you ever figure that out?"

Dinky sighed. "Okay, I'll show you again," he said. He took a piece of paper and a pencil. "To begin, you write out the first few letters of the message at the top of a sheet of paper like this":

WZ   VO   IZR   TJMF

"Then, under each letter, you simply run down the alphabet":

WZ	VO	IZR	TJMF
XA	WP	JAS	UKNG
YB	XQ	KBT	VLOH
ZC	YR	LCU	WMPI
AD	ZS	MDV	XNQJ
BE	AT	NEW	YORK
CF	BU	OFX	ZPSL
DG	CV	PGY	AQTM

"You usually don't have to run down the entire alphabet, just the first few letters. As you can see, the third line from the bottom contains the beginning of the clear message: 'BE AT NEW YORK.' Now, you're able to determine how many spaces the code alphabet has been moved over under the clear alphabet.

"First, you write down the clear alphabet":

A B C D E F G H I J K L M N O P Q R S T U V W X Y Z

"Then, if you go down the first column of letters, where we ran down the alphabet, you can see that 'W' in the code message is decoded by 'B' in the clear message. So under the letter 'B' in the clear alphabet, you write 'W' and continue with the other letters":

A B C D E F G H I J K L M N O P Q R S T U V W X Y Z
V W X Y Z A B C D E F G H I J K L M N O P Q R S T U

"Now you can see that the code alphabet has been moved over five spaces to the right under the clear alphabet. It's a simple matter, now, to decode the rest of the message."

"There's that word 'simple' again," Boris said. He looked hurt.

"I'm sorry," Dinky said. "What I meant is that it is now *possible* to decode the rest of the message. All you have to do is find each letter of the secret message in the code alphabet and look at the letter *above* it in the clear alphabet: 'CVMWJM' equals 'HARBOR,' 'VO' equals 'AT,' 'YVRI' equals 'DAWN,' 'VIY' equals 'AND,' 'OVFZ' equals 'TAKE,' 'KDXOPMZN' equals 'PICTURES,' 'JA' equals 'OF,' 'OCZ' equals 'THE,' 'VYHDMVG' equals 'ADMIRAL,' 'JCVMV' equals 'OHARA.' You never worry about apostrophes or periods or things like that. 'RCZI' equals 'WHEN,' 'DO' equals 'IT,' and 'NVDGN' equals 'SAILS.' "

"That's amazing," Boris said.

"It sure is," Wong agreed.

"Even I'm impressed," Lulu admitted.

"Well, I—" Dinky began.

"Say," Lulu interrupted, "isn't the *Admiral O'Hara* the newest ship in the American Navy?"

"Yes, it is," Boris said. "That's why we need the pictures. We don't have anything like it in our Navy. But oh, I dread that trip to New York. Why couldn't they want me to spy on something down here in Washington?" He sighed. "Well, I guess I'd better get started. I have to be in the Big Apple with my camera by dawn. Wish me luck!"

"Good luck," Wong said.

"Good luck," Lulu said.

"Yeah," Dinky added. But he looked concerned.

"Oh, my goodness, I almost forgot something," Boris said.

"What's that?" Dinky asked.

"I have to leave a message in another drop to let my contact know that I got this message. Will you help me with that one?"

"Sure," Dinky said.

"It'll cost you," Lulu said. "Remember, this is a business!"

"I think I still have a few *leva* left," Boris said.

"What do you want this message to say?" Dinky asked.

"I think it should sound very professional, don't you?" Boris said. "What about something like, *I got your message!*"

"Oh, boy, that really sounds professional," Lulu muttered.

"It needs to be in the same code as the last message," Boris added. "I do remember that much of what they told us at the Sofia Spy School."

"Why does it have to be in the same code?" Lulu asked.

"It's for our protection," Boris said. "It'll show my contact that I was able to decode his message. You see, these codes are so difficult that only highly trained Bulgarian spies such as myself are able to decode them."

"Oh, brother," Lulu said.

"Okay," Dinky began. "The last message used a variation of the Caesar Code. The code alphabet was moved over five spaces under the clear alphabet":

```
A B C D E F G H I J K L M N O P Q R S T U V W X Y Z
V W X Y Z A B C D E F G H I J K L M N O P Q R S T U
```

"So if we encode 'I GOT YOUR MESSAGE,' we'll have . . . we'll have . . . 'D BJO TJPM HZNNVBZ.' "

"Hmm," Boris mused, "I wonder if I should add anything else."

"How about *I'll take lots of good pictures of the Admiral O'Hara. You'll be proud of me,*" Lulu said.

"Not bad, not bad," Boris said. "You people certainly give good service here. I like that!"

Dinky began encoding the rest of the message: DGG OVFZ GJON JA BJJT KDXOPMZN JA OCZ VYHDM-VG JCVMV TJPGG WZ KMJPY JA HZ. When he finished, he handed it to Boris.

"Thanks a lot," Boris said. He took out his wallet. "Here are some more *leva*. If that's not enough, I'll be getting a lot more from Sofia soon."

"Oh, that's enough," Lulu said.

"Now, I'm supposed to leave this message at the drop in . . . uh, let me see . . . I think it's Dumbarton Oaks Park today . . . no, it's . . ." Boris thought real hard for a moment. "Oh, well, I'll leave it there anyway," he said. "I'm sure my contact will find it sooner or later. Then I have to catch the shuttle to New York. I

36

certainly hope that I can remember all of this. Well, I'll be seeing you around. And thanks again!''

Boris left the clubhouse and disappeared into the darkness.

''Boy, this has certainly been a busy day,'' Lulu said. ''I'm tired and hungry!''

''I am, too,'' Dinky said, ''and I still have to study for that English test.''

''Me, too,'' Wong added. Then he sighed deeply.

''What's wrong?'' Dinky asked.

''I guess I'm just like Lulu,'' Wong said. ''I'm worried about going to prison for helping Boris.''

''Worried?'' Lulu said. ''Did I say I was *worried?* I might not like prison, but that's the price you pay when you become a spy. I'm certainly not *worried!*''

''You know, we're not really helping Boris spy,'' Dinky said, ''we're just helping him *interpret* the secrets he's already obtained, that's all.''

''Hmm, I never thought about it that way,'' Wong said. ''But don't you think we ought at least to call the FBI or the CIA or *somebody* and tell them what we're doing?''

''How can we?'' Dinky said. ''If we do that, then we'll lose our credibility as the Secret Code Service. If people don't have complete trust in us, then they won't come to us with their secret messages.''

''Yeah,'' Lulu said, ''it's a definite problem all right.'' She yawned.

''It most certainly is,'' Dinky said.

''Well, what are we going to do about it?'' Wong asked.

''I'll have to think about it,'' Dinky said. ''But I'll have to come to a decision before dawn.''

''Why then?'' Wong asked.

''Because that's when the *Admiral O'Hara* sails from New York harbor,'' Dinky said.

"Oh, that's right," Wong said. "Well, let me know right away what your decision is."

"I personally don't mind if you wait until after eight o'clock to let me know your decision," Lulu said. "I'm usually not up at dawn." She put on her dark glasses and her beret. "See you in the morning, fellows!"

"I've got to go, too," Wong said. "I'll see you in English class."

"All right," Dinky said. "See you tomorrow."

Dinky sat down for a moment to think. Then he picked up his cryptology book, turned out the light, and went into the house.

"I think your dinner's all dried up, dear," Mrs. Lakewood said.

"Mother, would you still love me if I were sent to prison for treason?" Dinky asked.

"Of course I would, dear," Mrs. Lakewood said. "Now go wash your hands and I'll get your dinner out of the oven."

Dinky washed his hands and sat down at the table. His dinner *had* all dried up. The peas looked awful. They were all shriveled up. He was afraid to ask what kind of meat he was having. Actually, he decided, he wasn't as hungry as he had thought he was. "I think I'll go take a shower and study for my English test," he said.

"Well, all right, dear," Mrs. Lakewood said.

Mr. Lakewood was sitting in front of the television set, watching a rerun of a football game, when Dinky walked into the living room. "Dad, what happens to spies when they're caught?" he asked.

Mr. Lakewood looked up with bleary eyes. "They're shot, that's what!" he said. "They're taken out at dawn and shot between the eyes!" Then he went back to watching the rerun.

Dinky gulped. He felt worse. He went upstairs and

took a hot shower. Then he put on his pajamas and got into bed. He picked up his English book, then put it down. Why in the world should I study for an English test, he thought, if I'm going to be shot?

Dinky could see it all now. There would be police knocking at the door. He'd be taken away in a paddy wagon with all the neighbors watching. There would be newspaper headlines and the trial and prison and then, in the cold dawn, they'd march him outside, blindfold him, and . . .

BANG! BANG! BANG!

Dinky sat up with a start. Was he already dead? No, his heart was pounding. He couldn't be dead.

BANG! BANG! BANG!

"Dinky? Are you in there?" It was his dad, knocking at the door.

Dinky could hardly speak. Finally, he was able to say, "Yes, I'm in here, what is it?"

"There's somebody downstairs to see you," Mr. Lakewood answered.

"Who is it?" Dinky asked.

"I don't know, but he looks important," Mr. Lakewood said. "What have you been up to?"

Dinky got out of bed. "Just a minute, Dad," he said. He went to the window and looked out. A long, black limousine was parked in front of the house. He began to break out in a cold sweat. Oh, no, he thought, this is the end. They've come for me. I'm not ready to die. He sighed deeply. But at least it wasn't a paddy wagon parked in front. Maybe it wouldn't look too bad to the neighbors when they hauled him away. He walked to the door. "I'll get dressed now, Dad," he whispered.

"Well, all right, but hurry!" Mr. Lakewood shouted back.

I have to be dignified, Dinky thought. I can't scream and yell and carry on. When Mom and Dad look back on this night in years to come, they'll be proud of the way I acted when they carried me away.

Dinky put on his best jeans and his best shirt. He even combed his hair. He looked around his room. There were books he wanted to read, model airplanes he wanted to glue together . . . maybe they'd let him do some of those things in prison while he was waiting to be . . . shot.

He opened the door to his room and started down the stairs.

When he reached the living room, his father said, "Dinky, this is Mr. Willowbrook. He's from the State Department. He wants to talk to you."

Mr. Willowbrook wasn't smiling. But he wasn't frowning, either. He was alone, too. And he didn't have a gun or handcuffs.

"You wanted to see me?" Dinky said. He could feel his voice quivering.

"Yes, yes, I do," Mr. Willowbrook said. He looked around the room, then directly at Mr. and Mrs. Lakewood. "Could we possibly discuss this in private?"

"Oh, certainly, certainly," Mr. Lakewood said sarcastically. "I don't have to know how this incredibly exciting football game is going to turn out!"

"I suppose I could go out into the kitchen and bake some pies," Mrs. Lakewood said.

"That's all right," Dinky said. "I'll get my flashlight and we can go out to the clubhouse. That'll be private."

Dinky got his flashlight, and Mr. Willowbrook followed him out to the clubhouse. Dinky turned on the light, and Mr. Willowbrook sat down.

"This is nice," Mr. Willowbrook said. "Is this where you do most of your work?"

"Work?" Dinky said. He was trying to be cautious.

Mr. Willowbrook held up a piece of paper. "Yes," he said, "your Secret Code Service work."

"How did you know about that?" Dinky asked.

"One of my assistants found your advertisement on a bus yesterday," Mr. Willowbrook explained. "He gave it to me. You see, I'm Head of the Cryptology Section at the Department of State."

"Oh, well," Dinky said, "I'm really sorry if—"

"The problem is," Mr. Willowbrook continued, "we intercepted a secret message tonight that neither I nor any of my assistants can decode. I remembered your advertisement, and I thought you might be able to help us. I just have a feeling that this message is extremely important."

"Well, I'll certainly try," Dinky said.

Mr. Willowbrook took out a folded piece of paper from his briefcase, unfolded it, and handed it to Dinky.

Dinky looked at it. He was shocked. But he tried not to show it. He was holding the same message that he had encoded for Boris earlier in the evening! "Where did you get this?" he asked.

"I'm afraid I cannot reveal my source," Mr. Willowbrook said.

Dinky was beginning to get his composure back. "Mr. Willowbrook," he said, "the Secret Code Service prides itself on its integrity. We have clients from all over the world who come to us for encoding and decoding. They trust us completely. Our motto is: 'Your Secrets Are Our Secrets!' "

"Oh, all right," Mr. Willowbrook said. "Well, we've been following this Bulgarian spy for months. He was arrested tonight in Dumbarton Oaks Park."

Dinky gasped. "Did he have a red nose?" he asked.

"A *what?*" Mr. Willowbrook said. "No, no, he didn't." He looked puzzled. "Well, anyway, we found this secret message on him that we've not been able to decode. It's extremely complicated. I doubt if you'll be able to solve it, but I thought I'd at least give your organization a chance."

"Well, it does look rather complicated," Dinky said, "but I'll try. Oh, by the way, we usually fill out personal information cards on all our clients for our files. Would you mind . . ."

Mr. Willowbrook frowned.

". . . But it's late," Dinky continued, "so I guess we'll just dispense with that for now. You just sit back, relax, and read a magazine. I'll see what I can do with this message."

Mr. Willowbrook picked up a copy of *Congressional Record* and started reading. "I'm impressed with your waiting room magazines," he said.

Dinky smiled pleasantly. Then he sat down at his desk and put the coded message in front of him.

"Oh, Mr. Lakewood! Mr. Lakewood!"

Mr. Willowbrook looked up. "What was that?"

"I don't believe it," Dinky muttered. "I just don't believe it!"

"There you are, Mr. Lakewood." Emma shined her flashlight through the door of the clubhouse. "I thought I'd find you here."

"Emma, please," Dinky pleaded. "I'm busy. Can't you come back some other time?"

"No, I cannot, Mr. Lakewood," Emma said. "I indeed cannot. Ethel broke that code you thought was unbreakable. And I am holding you to your promise of my money back or a brand-new code!"

"Who *is* this woman?" Mr. Willowbrook said.

"She's a client of ours," Dinky explained. He looked back at Emma. "I'm really very busy now, Emma, can't you see?"

"I'll wait," Emma said. "Good evening, young man," she said to Mr. Willowbrook.

Mr. Willowbrook nodded. "Good evening."

42

"Do you mind if Emma stays, Mr. Willowbrook?" Dinky asked.

"I guess not," Mr. Willowbrook said. He smiled. "As long as she's not a spy," he added.

"My sister's a spy," Emma said.

Mr. Willowbrook's head jerked up. "She is?" he gasped.

"No, she's really not," Dinky said hurriedly. "She just keeps breaking the codes that Emma uses in her diary, that's all."

"She's unscrupulous," Emma said, "and she's headed for a life of crime. She'll be in prison before she's eighty!"

"Please, Emma," Dinky said, "just sit in your chair and . . . did you bring your knitting?"

"Yes, I did," Emma said.

"Good," Dinky said. "Just sit there and knit! Now, then, Mr. Willowbrook, as I was saying . . ." Dinky looked up. Mr. Willowbrook was obviously getting very nervous. He knew he'd better hurry up and not pretend to take too much time. He looked back down at the secret message. ". . . Well, I think it might be . . . yes, yes . . . I'm getting it . . . I'm decoding it in my head . . . yes, this makes sense . . . it's coming . . . I've got it!"

"Good heavens, man, is this the way you work?" Mr. Willowbrook said. "You must be fantastic!"

"I try very hard," Dinky said.

"You should see . . . knit one, purl two . . . my sister Ethel," Emma said.

"Well, what does the message say?" Mr. Willowbrook demanded.

Dinky took a deep breath. "It says, 'I GOT YOUR MESSAGE. I'LL TAKE LOTS OF GOOD PICTURES OF THE ADMIRAL O'HARA. YOU'LL BE PROUD OF ME.' "

"I knew that message would be important," Mr. Willowbrook shouted, "I just knew it! The *Admiral O'Hara* sails at dawn from New York harbor. We'll have men up there to catch that spy. He'll never take any pictures! How much do I owe you?"

"Five dollars," Emma said.

Mr. Willowbrook handed Dinky five dollars. "You've done your government a great service," he said. "And I can tell you one thing, I won't forget this. If I ever need any more help, I'll be back. You're fantastic!"

Dinky blushed. "Thanks," he said.

"Good evening, ma'am," Mr. Willowbrook said to Emma.

"Good evening, young man," Emma said.

Dinky sat down.

"And now . . . knit one, purl two . . . my code, please," Emma said pointedly.

"Oh, Emma, I'm so tired," Dinky said. "Do you plan to write any more in your diary tonight?"

"Well, no, I don't . . ." Emma said.

"Then why don't you just let me think about it overnight," Dinky said, "and I'm sure that I can come up with something that Ethel will never be able to figure out."

"Well, all right," Emma said. "But I'll be over here tomorrow just as soon as you get home from school, and I'll expect a supercode!"

"Agreed," Dinky said.

He helped Emma to the gate and said good night. Then he collapsed against the fence. He wasn't going to be shot after all. In fact, right now, in the eyes of the government, he was a hero.

But Dinky was still concerned. Now, he wondered, what in the world was going to happen to Boris?

Chapter Five

Monday morning, Dinky had so much on his mind that he found it difficult on the English test to tell the difference between a verb and a noun.

"Next year, pupils," Miss Barberton droned on as the class began handing in their examination papers, "when you have to start diagramming, you'll regret not having studied in this class!"

Dinky dreaded diagramming. And to hear Miss Barberton talk, diagramming was necessary to life itself.

At lunch, in the school cafeteria, the three members of the Secret Code Service sat together, huddled at a corner table.

"I had a visit from the State Department last night," Dinky announced.

"Really?" Wong said. "Did they come to arrest you?"

"I don't think the State Department ever arrests anybody," Lulu said between bites of mashed potatoes. "You're thinking about the FBI."

"What'd they want, then?" Wong said.

"It was a Mr. Willowbrook," Dinky explained, "and he had the secret message that we had encoded for Boris, the one about taking pictures of the *Admiral O'Hara.*"

"Really?" Wong and Lulu said in unison.

"How'd he get it?" Lulu asked.

"Well, it seems they've been following Boris's contact for months," Dinky said. "He was arrested last night when he picked up the message that Boris had left at the drop in Dumbarton Oaks Park."

"Oh, no!" Wong exclaimed.

"Did they get Boris, too?" Lulu asked.

"No," Dinky said. "I don't think they even saw him. In fact, I don't think they even know what he looks like."

Wong and Lulu breathed a sigh of relief.

"Do you think Boris knows that his contact was arrested?" Lulu asked.

"I don't think so," Dinky said.

"Do you think that we should tell him?" Wong said.

"We can't," Dinky said. "We cannot compromise the integrity of the Secret Code Service."

"Did you decode the message for Mr. Willowbrook?" Lulu asked.

"Of course I did," Dinky said. He took a bite of green beans. "He came to me with a secret message that he wanted decoded, and I decoded it for him."

"Gee, you must be better at this than I thought you were," Wong said.

"Did this Willowbrook fellow pay you?" Lulu asked.

"Certainly," Dinky said. "Five dollars!"

Lulu's eyes gleamed.

"Did you tell him that you—pass the butter, please—were the one who had encoded it in the first place?" Wong asked.

"Of course not," Dinky said. "That would have betrayed Boris's trust in me."

"Well, now that the State Department knows somebody is going to New York to take pictures of the

Admiral O'Hara, I guess you don't have to worry anymore about committing treason,'' Lulu said.

"I guess not," Dinky said. He thought for a minute. "Then why am I so depressed?"

"I don't know," Lulu said, "but so am I."

"Me, too," Wong agreed.

They all sighed deeply.

"Where do we go from here?" Lulu said finally.

"We sit and wait," Dinky said.

"Do you think the State Department notified the FBI?" Wong asked.

"Probably," Dinky said.

"Then that'll be the end of Boris," Lulu said with another sigh. "I hear the FBI always gets its man."

"Poor Boris," Dinky said. "I kind of liked him."

"Who'd have thought that we'd ever become so attached to our clients?" Wong said sadly.

"Well, life goes on," Lulu said philosophically. "I came to terms with that myself the day I decided to become a spy. I know that if I'm captured, my government will deny that I ever existed and I'll be hanged!"

Dinky and Wong gulped. *"Hanged?"* they said.

Lulu nodded.

All three sighed deeply again.

Then Lulu began buttering a piece of bread. "Well," she said brightly, "what are we going to do with all this money we're making?"

"I'm appointing Wong Treasurer," Dinky said. "He can take— "

"Wait a minute," Lulu interrupted, "just wait a minute! I thought you had appointed me Head of the International Banking Department!"

"I did," Dinky said, "but I've decided that you're much too valuable to the Cryptology Section of this organization to be spared."

"Well, you're right about that," Lulu said.

"Wong, I want you to take the money to the bank today and open up an account," Dinky said.

"Where's the money?" Wong asked.

"I have it in my wallet," Dinky said. He took out his wallet and handed the money to Wong. "It's almost time for class. Lulu and I'll be at the clubhouse after school. We have some business to take care of. Come straight there from the bank."

"What business?" Lulu asked.

"We have to make up another secret code for Emma," Dinky said.

"Don't tell me Ethel figured out the second one, too?" Lulu said.

"It didn't take her as long as the first one," Dinky said dejectedly.

"It sounds to me as if we should ask Ethel to join the Secret Code Service," Wong said.

Dinky thought for a minute. "That might not be such a bad idea," he said. "Come on, let's put away our trays."

After school, Dinky and Lulu walked straight to the clubhouse.

Emma was waiting for them. "Are you ready with a new code, or do I get my money back?" she asked.

"I'll give you a new code," Dinky said.

"Good," Emma said, "because I've written a lot of things that I don't want Ethel to find out about!"

Lulu sat down in the back of the clubhouse and started reading *How to Be a Spy*.

Dinky opened up his codebook and started looking. "We might try a transposition code," he said after a few minutes.

"I'll try anything to keep Ethel from discovering my secrets," Emma said.

"Let me see what you've written today," Dinky said.

Emma reluctantly handed Dinky a sheet of paper.

"Is this it?" Dinky said. "There are only two sentences on this sheet of paper."

"Yes, I know," Emma said. "But if that information ever got out, my reputation would be ruined!"

Dinky read the two sentences aloud: *"I no longer love Dr. Bellflower. I love his rival, Dr. Redondo, instead."*

Lulu snorted from behind her book.

"Professionalism!" Dinky shouted.

"Sorry," Lulu muttered.

"Okay," Dinky began, "what we need to do is this. We'll write out the clear message on a sheet of paper and number the letters":

```
1    2 3    4 5 6 7 8 9    10 11 12 13    14 15    16 17 18 19
I    N O    L O N G E R    L  O  V  E     D  R.    B  E  L  L-

20 21 22 23 24 25    26    27 28 29 30    31 32 33    34 35 36 37 38
F  L  O  W  E  R.     I    L  O  V  E     H  I  S     R  I  V  A  L,

39 40    41 42 43 44 45 46 47    48 49 50 51 52 53 54
D  R.    R  E  D  O  N  D  O,    I  N  S  T  E  A  D.
```

"Then we'll write the odd-numbered letters on the top line and the even-numbered letters on the bottom line. It'll look like this." Dinky finished writing:

```
I O O G R O E R E L L W R L V H S I A D R D N O N T A
N L N E L V D B L F O E I O E I R V L R E O D I S E D
```

"That's wonderful," Emma said.

"Let me see," Lulu said. She looked at the code. "If Ethel can figure that out, then we definitely need to make her an offer!"

"An offer?" Emma said.

"Since Ethel's so good at decoding secret messages,"

Dinky said, "we thought we might ask her to join the Secret Code Service."

"Well, at least it'd get her out of the house," Emma said. "She's driving me and Momma crazy!"

"It was just an idea we had," Dinky added. "We haven't reached a firm decision yet."

"All right," Emma said. "Well, I'll take this code home and try it, but if Ethel figures this one out, too, then I'm coming straight back here!"

"Our work is always guaranteed," Dinky said.

Emma left the clubhouse, muttering about how unscrupulous Ethel was.

"I almost hope Ethel breaks that code," Lulu said.

"Why, for goodness sakes?" Dinky said.

"I think we could use a mind like Ethel's in this operation," Lulu said.

Wong appeared in the doorway. "Emma certainly looked happy," he said. "Did you get her a new code?"

"Yes, but I have a feeling that Ethel will break this one, too," Dinky said.

"I definitely think that Ethel would be an asset to the Secret Code Service," Lulu said.

"Let's have your Treasurer's report," Dinky said, making way for Wong to come inside.

Wong took out a spiral notebook and began reading. "The Secret Code Service now has a bank account balance of ten American dollars and forty Bulgarian *leva*."

"*Ten* American dollars!" Dinky said. "I thought I gave you fifteen!"

"You did," Wong said patiently. He turned to Lulu. "Here's the five dollars the Secret Code Service owes you for bus fare."

Lulu raised an eyebrow. "It's about time," she said. "I thought I was going to have to turn it over to a collection agency."

"Oh, I'd forgotten about that," Dinky said. "But what about those *leva,* couldn't you get them changed into dollars?"

"The man at the bank said he'd work on it," Wong answered. "They don't seem to get many *leva* these days. He wasn't quite sure what the exchange rate was."

"Maybe we shouldn't exchange them," Lulu said. "I may need them in case I ever have to slip undercover into Bulgaria."

"Anybody home?"

They all three looked up. Boris was standing in the doorway.

"Boris!" Lulu shouted.

"We thought you had been capt . . ." Dinky started to say but thought better of it.

"What are you doing here?" Wong finally asked.

"Oh, I missed the shuttle to New York, and I couldn't get a seat on the next one and . . ." Boris came inside and sat down. ". . . And you know, it was just one thing after another. By the time I was finally able to get a seat, it was too late to make it to New York by dawn, so I just told them to forget it. Boy, am I ever glad to sit down. I've been walking all over Washington all afternoon, trying to contact my contact."

Lulu started coughing.

Wong flushed.

Dinky turned pale.

But nobody said anything.

"And I'm worried, too," Boris continued. "I think he may have been arrested."

"I thought you didn't know who your contact was," Lulu said. "How would you be able to recognize him?"

"I *don't* know who he is," Boris said. "I've never seen him before. But I'd be able to recognize him anywhere. We're all given the same clothes to wear and the same instructions on how to act as a spy. He'd stand out in a crowd.''

"Do you, uh, plan to keep looking for him?'' Dinky asked.

"No, I'm too tired,'' Boris said. He took off his shoes and began massaging his feet. "But I do think I ought to leave him a message, though—just in case. I need to let him know that I never made it to New York.'' Boris handed Dinky the copy of *All the Bulgarian Codes You'll Ever Need!* "Could you find something in there that I could use?'' he asked.

Dinky took the codebook and started turning the pages. "Here's something that would be good,'' he said.

"Okay, I'll take your word for it,'' Boris said. "Here's the message I want encoded: *Missed the boat in New York. What time does the next one sail?''*

"All right,'' Dinky began. "This is Trithemius's Square Table. It consists of twenty-six alphabets, each one being slid one place to the left of the previous one. The table looks like this'':

```
A B C D E F G H I J K L M N O P Q R S T U V W X Y Z
B C D E F G H I J K L M N O P Q R S T U V W X Y Z A
C D E F G H I J K L M N O P Q R S T U V W X Y Z A B
D E F G H I J K L M N O P Q R S T U V W X Y Z A B C
E F G H I J K L M N O P Q R S T U V W X Y Z A B C D
F G H I J K L M N O P Q R S T U V W X Y Z A B C D E
G H I J K L M N O P Q R S T U V W X Y Z A B C D E F
H I J K L M N O P Q R S T U V W X Y Z A B C D E F G
I J K L M N O P Q R S T U V W X Y Z A B C D E F G H
J K L M N O P Q R S T U V W X Y Z A B C D E F G H I
K L M N O P Q R S T U V W X Y Z A B C D E F G H I J
L M N O P Q R S T U V W X Y Z A B C D E F G H I J K
M N O P Q R S T U V W X Y Z A B C D E F G H I J K L
N O P Q R S T U V W X Y Z A B C D E F G H I J K L M
O P Q R S T U V W X Y Z A B C D E F G H I J K L M N
P Q R S T U V W X Y Z A B C D E F G H I J K L M N O
Q R S T U V W X Y Z A B C D E F G H I J K L M N O P
R S T U V W X Y Z A B C D E F G H I J K L M N O P Q
S T U V W X Y Z A B C D E F G H I J K L M N O P Q R
T U V W X Y Z A B C D E F G H I J K L M N O P Q R S
U V W X Y Z A B C D E F G H I J K L M N O P Q R S T
V W X Y Z A B C D E F G H I J K L M N O P Q R S T U
W X Y Z A B C D E F G H I J K L M N O P Q R S T U V
X Y Z A B C D E F G H I J K L M N O P Q R S T U V W
Y Z A B C D E F G H I J K L M N O P Q R S T U V W X
Z A B C D E F G H I J K L M N O P Q R S T U V W X Y
```

"Now, then," he continued, "the message you want to encode is: 'MISSED THE BOAT IN NEW YORK. WHAT TIME DOES THE NEXT ONE SAIL?' We'll use each alphabet to encode succeeding letters of the message. In other words, the first letter of the message, 'M,' will be encoded by the first alphabet, which is also the clear alphabet. So, 'M' will remain 'M.' The second letter in the message is 'I.' Find 'I' in the first alphabet and look below it in the second alphabet. You'll see that 'I' will be encoded by the letter 'J.' The third letter of the message is 'S.' Again, find 'S' in the first alphabet and look below it in the third alphabet. 'S' will be encoded by the letter 'U.' The fourth letter is also 'S,' but this 'S' will be encoded by using the fourth alpha- bet, so 'S' equals 'V'. 'E' equals 'I,' and 'D' equals

'I.' 'MISSED,' then, is encoded as 'MJUVII.' Now, if we do this with the rest of the message, we'll have . . .'' Dinky closed his eyes. ''. . . We'll have MJUVII ZOM KYLF VB CUN QHLF SEYS TJOH HTKZ BQO YQKH DDV KTCG.''

"That looks great," Boris said. "I just hope my contact finds it in time, or they're really going to be mad in Sofia because I didn't take those pictures."

"Will you get into trouble?" Lulu asked.

"Who knows?" Boris said. He thought for a minute. "Maybe I could fake something."

Lulu gasped. "How unprofessional!" she said.

"No, no," Boris said, "it's done all the time." He put his shoes back on. "Oh, my feet still hurt! How much do I owe you for this message?"

"Well—" Dinky began.

"I think I paid you about five *leva* for the last one, didn't I?" Boris interrupted.

"That's fine," Dinky said.

"Oh, by the way, Boris," Wong spoke up, "how much is a *lev* worth in American money?"

"Gee," Boris said, "I'm not quite sure. I'll try to find out for you, though. Well, I'd better be on my way. Today's Tuesday, so I have to leave the message in—"

"Today's Monday, Boris," Lulu interrupted.

"Monday! Are you sure?" Boris said.

"I'm positive," Dinky said. "We always have an English test on Monday."

"Monday, now let's see," Boris mused aloud, "which park is it on Monday . . . oh, yes, it's Montrose Park. I think. Well, anyway, I'll try that one. See you guys later!"

" 'Bye, Boris," they all said in unison.

"You know," Lulu said after Boris had left, "it's a good thing we don't have to send in evaluation reports on the different spies we handle."

"Yeah," Dinky agreed. "Poor Boris wouldn't receive a very high rating."

"Say," Wong said, "how'd you two do on that English test?"

"Don't ask," Dinky said.

"I wrote some of my answers in code," Lulu said. "That always impresses Miss Barberton."

"Oh, Mr. Lakewood! It's me, Mr. Lakewood!" Emma opened the door of the clubhouse. Standing next to her was another elderly lady. She was dressed in a red cowgirl outfit covered with sequins and rhinestones. With her left hand, she was twirling a lasso.

"Who's your friend, Emma?" Lulu asked.

"Her? She's no friend of mine," Emma said with a pout. "She's my little sister, Ethel."

"Hi, gang!" Ethel shouted. She stuck out her right hand to Dinky. "Put 'er there!" she said. She continued to twirl the lasso with her left hand.

"I like your outfit," Lulu said.

"Yeah? Well, the rodeo is in town and I'm thinkin' about joinin' up, girlie," Ethel said proudly. "That's why I'm practicin' all these tricks with my lasso here."

"Disgraceful!" Emma muttered. "Unscrupulous!"

"You're an old fuddy-duddy, Emma," Ethel said. She slapped her sister across the back with her free hand and sent her flying into a chair. "You gotta live, Emma, live, live!" Turning back to Dinky, she added, "Now, what's this about me joinin' up with you?"

"Don't tell me you broke that last code, too!" Dinky said.

"Of course I did!" Ethel boasted. "I've always been able to figure out things!"

"Well, we were thinking that you might like to be a member of the Secret Code Service," Dinky said, "seeing as how you've been able to break all the codes we've given Emma."

"We sure could use your brain," Lulu added.

"You certainly have a definite ability to solve codes," Wong said.

"You're right there, sonny," Ethel said. "Nobody's ever been able to keep a secret from me!" She looked directly at Emma.

"You'll be in prison before you're eighty!" Emma said with a cough.

"They'll have to catch me first," Ethel shouted at her.

"Now, girls," Lulu said, "let's have none of that bickering!"

KNOCK! KNOCK! KNOCK! KNOCK!

Everybody looked up just as the door opened. It was Mr. Willowbrook.

"Come on in, Mr. Willowbrook," Dinky said.

Mr. Willowbrook remained standing at the door. "I'd like to talk to you in private, Mr. Lakewood," he said.

"Oh, you don't have to worry about these people," Dinky said. He offered Mr. Willowbrook a chair. "Everybody in here belongs in here."

Mr. Willowbrook came inside, but he didn't sit down.

"You remember Emma from last night, don't you, Mr. Willowbrook?" Dinky said.

"Charmed, I'm sure," Emma said. "Are you married?"

"Uh, yes, as a matter of fact, I am," Mr. Willowbrook stammered. "Happily!"

"Too bad," Emma said.

"And this is her little sister, Ethel," Dinky continued. "She's a brilliant cryptologist. We've just offered her a position with the Secret Code Service."

"Yeah, but I may be joinin' the rodeo instead," Ethel said. "I'm still tryin' to make up my mind."

"She'll be in prison before she's eighty," Emma muttered.

"And this is our Treasurer, Wong Chiang," Dinky added, "and another brilliant cryptologist, Lulu Hawthorne."

Lulu curtsied.

Mr. Willowbrook looked stunned. "This is quite an organization," he managed to say. "Well," he continued, sitting down, "if everybody here belongs here, then I guess that I have no objections."

"Now, then, what was it you wanted to talk to us about?" Dinky said.

Mr. Willowbrook opened his briefcase. "I told you about the spy we captured in Dumbarton Oaks Park Sunday night," Mr. Willowbrook said. "Well, we finally made him talk!"

Lulu inhaled sharply. Mr. Willowbrook looked at her. "Bronchitis," Lulu said quickly.

"As I was saying," Mr. Willowbrook continued, "we finally made him talk. We now know that his contact is a very dangerous man, a spy whose very existence poses a threat to Western Civilization as we know it."

"Heavens!" Emma said.

"Good gracious!" Ethel said.

"Why are you telling *us* this?" Dinky asked.

"Because we want your organization to help us capture him," Mr. Willowbrook said.

Dinky's heart skipped a beat. "What's this man's name?" he asked.

Mr. Willowbrook paused, looked around the clubhouse, then set his jaw. "We know him as Boris the Bad Bulgarian," he whispered.

Chapter Six

"Did the spy you captured tell you anything else?" Dinky asked.

Wong and Lulu looked apprehensive.

"Yes, we learned several things," Mr. Willowbrook said. "For one, he told us where to find the next message. It was in Montrose Park. But we can't decode this one, either. I thought maybe you could." He handed the message to Dinky.

Dinky tried to remain calm. Lulu and Wong crowded around him.

"Why, isn't that the same mes—" Wong started to say, but Lulu stepped on his toes. "—Ouch!"

"Of course, we'll certainly try, Mr. Willowbrook," Dinky said, trying to sound noncommittal. "When did you need it decoded?"

"How about yesterday," Mr. Willowbrook said. He smiled. "Look, Mr. Lakewood," he continued, "I appreciate the fact that you are a very busy man." He stopped and looked around the clubhouse. "But this could mean life or death for this country . . . this planet . . . this universe . . . this—"

"Okay, okay," Lulu said, "we get the message!"

Mr. Willowbrook took a deep breath. "We are talking," he concluded, "about a spy whose very existence threatens Western Civilization as we know it!"

"Well, in that case . . ." Dinky said. He pretended to study the message. "Yes, yes, I think it is . . . of course, just a minute now, I'm getting it. Yes, this is a message which uses Trithemius's Square Table. Of course, I have the table committed to memory, so all I need to do is close my eyes and . . . and . . . I've got it: 'MISSED THE BOAT IN NEW YORK. WHAT TIME DOES THE NEXT ONE SAIL?' "

"Very clever," Mr. Willowbrook said. "Very, very clever!"

Dinky blushed. "Thank you very much," he said.

"What? Oh! Actually, I was talking about Boris the Bad Bulgarian," Mr. Willowbrook said. "But you were good, too, Mr. Lakewood, very good. We'll talk about your future later. Right now, I'm more interested in this Boris fellow. Don't you see how brilliant the man is? He knew we were after him. He knew that there would be agents in New York when the *Admiral O'Hara* sailed. So he never went! We're working with a mastermind, Mr. Lakewood, a mastermind of treachery!"

"Oh, brother," Lulu muttered.

"I can feel it, Mr. Lakewood." Mr. Willowbrook extended his arms. "I think we're close to capturing this man Boris. With your help, we should have him behind bars in a few days."

"The cost will be high," Lulu said.

Mr. Willowbrook turned. "We're prepared to pay any price," he said. He looked back at Dinky. "Is your organization up to the task?"

"We'll do our part," Dinky said. "We'll do whatever encoding and decoding you hire us to do."

"Then you will be mentioned prominently in my report to the Secretary of State," Mr. Willowbrook said. "Now, here's what I want you to encode." He wrote out a message on a piece of paper, then handed it to Dinky.

Dinky read the message. "Don't you think this is a little obvious?" he said. "Don't you think that Boris will expect danger?"

Mr. Willowbrook beamed. "That's just the point," he said. "It will seem so outrageous that he'll think it's real!"

"Well, whatever you say," Dinky conceded. "You're paying for it." He got out a pencil and a piece of paper.

"Oh, yes, I almost forgot," Mr. Willowbrook said. "Be sure and put it in the same code as the last one, that Tri*whatever* Square Table you mentioned. These Bulgarian spies always put their replies in the same code as the previous message. That's something else we learned from the man we captured!"

"Trithemius's Square Table," Dinky said.

"That's it," Mr. Willowbrook said.

Dinky began encoding the message. Wong and Lulu huddled around him and watched.

Mr. Willowbrook sat in silence. Emma kept winking at him.

Ethel began practicing her rope tricks again.

Finally, Dinky had finished encoding the message. He handed it to Mr. Willowbrook.

"Thank you," Mr. Willowbrook said. "Your government owes you a debt of gratitude."

"And five dollars!" Lulu added.

"Oh, yes, I almost forgot," Mr. Willowbrook said. He took out his wallet and handed Dinky a five-dollar bill. Dinky handed it to Wong. "I'll need a receipt," Mr. Willowbrook added.

"Well, I don't—" Dinky began.

But Lulu interrupted. "Our receipt books are still at

60

the printer's," she said. "I'll make out one and give it to you next time."

"There may not be a next time," Mr. Willowbrook said. His eyes were gleaming. "I'm taking this to a drop right now!"

"Do you know where to put the next message?" Dinky asked.

"Well, not exactly," Mr. Willowbrook admitted. "You see, the spy we captured usually receives a list of which parks to use from the Sofia Spy School, but evidently there's a postal strike in Bulgaria and the list hasn't arrived yet."

"Well, well, well," Lulu said, "it looks as though Boris the Bad Bulgarian might not be taken after all."

Mr. Willowbrook smiled enigmatically. "Oh, yes, he will," he said. "We've thought of everything. We plan to put this message in *all* the parks in Washington. We'll have Boris the Bad Bulgarian before the day is up!"

"I wouldn't count on it," Lulu said.

But Mr. Willowbrook was already headed out the door.

After she was sure that Mr. Willowbrook was gone and couldn't hear her, Lulu said, "Boris? A dangerous spy? They've got to be kidding!"

"That's what I was thinking, too," Wong added.

Dinky turned to Ethel. "We sure could use an unbiased opinion," he said. "Would you be willing to observe Boris for a period of time and then report to us?"

"What do you mean?" Ethel asked.

"We think Boris is nice, if somewhat, well, uh, *thick* at times," Lulu said, "but Mr. Willowbrook seems to think he's a threat to civilization."

"I gathered as much," Ethel said. "Well, I am a pretty good judge of character. I'll give it my best shot."

"Thanks, Ethel," Dinky said.

"Don't mention it," Ethel said. "Now, then, let's get back to my career!"

"Oh, yeah, well, uh, we three, that is, the members of the Secret Code Service talked it over, and we were thinking about offering you a position on our staff," Dinky said.

"We sure could use someone with your ability," Lulu said.

"Do you have a policy of hiring criminals?" Emma asked.

Ethel turned to rope Emma with her lasso.

But Dinky stopped her. "What do you say, Ethel, are you interested?" he asked hurriedly.

"Well, I want to talk to the Rodeo Boss first," Ethel said. "Actually, I kind of have a hankerin' to go out West, where the buffalo roam and the deer and the antelope play. Where seldom is heard—"

"All right!" Emma shouted. She turned to Dinky. "She's only been talking like that since the rodeo came to town. It's disgraceful!"

"You could still toss me a few secret messages from time to time," Ethel said, "whenever you get stumped."

"We try not to toss around the secret messages we get," Dinky explained patiently.

"You'd be wasting your talents in the rodeo," Lulu said. "You could be a brilliant cryptologist. Just like me."

"I know, I know," Ethel said. "But honey, I've always wanted to be a cowgirl, and this is my chance!"

"I'm leaving," Emma said, "and I'm going to tell Momma how you've been behaving, too!"

Ethel made a face as Emma toddled out the clubhouse door. "Never was any fun, that one!" she said.

"Dinky! Dinky Lakewood!"

"It's Mom," Dinky said. He stuck his head outside the door. "Yes, ma'am?"

"Would you and your friends like some sandwiches and milk?"

"That sounds good," Dinky shouted back. "Thanks!"

"Sandwiches and milk," Lulu muttered. "When are we going to graduate to champagne and caviar, like real spies?"

Mrs. Lakewood brought out a tray piled high with sandwiches and a large pitcher of milk. For the next fifteen minutes, everyone concentrated on eating. Lulu was just about to send Dinky back to the house for some more sandwiches when the door of the clubhouse opened.

"Yoohoo!"

Everybody looked up. A very tired-looking Boris was standing in the doorway.

"Boris!" Dinky shouted.

Ethel took one look at Boris and said, "Oh, you poor, poor dear! Come in and sit down. Here! Finish the rest of my sandwich."

Lulu, Wong, and Dinky looked at each other.

"Isn't that a rather snap judgment on your part?" Dinky said.

"Not at all," Ethel replied. "I can take one look at a person and immediately tell what he's like."

Boris sat down next to Ethel and started eating the sandwich. "This is good," he said. "I was really getting hungry."

"I knew you were," Ethel said. She patted the top of Boris's head. "I knew you were."

"Who *are* you?" Boris asked.

"Just call me Ethel," Ethel said.

"Are you a cowgirl?" Boris asked.

"I may be," Ethel replied.

"I've always wanted to go out West and ride horses," Boris confessed. "I never really wanted to be a spy, even though I am exceptionally well trained."

"Well, then why don't we just do it?" Ethel said. "Why don't we just stop all this spy nonsense and go out to Texas? I can buy a ranch, and you can be my foreman."

"I don't know," Boris said. "This is all so sudden."

"I know, I know," Ethel said. "But life's funny that way."

"It is, isn't it?" Boris declared. "But spying is all I know. Do you think I could get a job in Texas as a spy until I learned how to be a ranch foreman?"

"Well, I'm sure they have jobs for spies in Texas," Ethel said, "especially if you could get some good recommendations."

"I'd give you a good recommendation, Boris," Lulu said.

"So would I," Dinky said.

"Me, too," Wong added.

"Well, you know, I just might . . ." Boris hesitated. "I think I'm . . ."

"Yes? Yes?" Ethel said breathlessly.

"Let me take care of this last meeting first," Boris said, "and then we'll be on our way to Texas!"

"You'll never regret this decision," Ethel said.

"Wait a minute," Dinky said. "What meeting?"

"Oh, I forgot to tell you," Boris said. "I found a message in Davies Park." He took a piece of paper out of his pocket and unfolded it. "I'm sure it has something to do with a face-to-face meeting. If I could just get you to decode this one last message for me . . . and I'm afraid that I don't have any more *leva* . . ."

"That's okay," Wong said. "We have more than enough already."

". . . Then I could follow the instructions and meet my contact," Boris continued. "I want to give him a message to take back to the folks in Sofia. Then I'd be free to go to Texas with Ethel."

"Are you sure you want to do this?" Dinky said. "Why don't you just forget about the message and go on to Texas?"

"I'm too highly trained to do that," Boris declared. "Besides, I think I owe it to my teachers at the Sofia Spy School to tell them that . . . that . . ." He began blushing. ". . . That I cheated when I was in school and that it's not really their fault that I've been such a . . . yes, I'm man enough to admit it . . . a failure!"

"But Boris," Lulu protested, "if you have this meeting, then . . ."

Dinky raised his hand for silence. "If Boris has made his decision, then he has made his decision," he said. "It is not for the members of the Secret Code Service to interfere with the lives of its clients—even if we do like some of them better than others. Boris, let me see the message."

Boris handed the message to Dinky.

Dinky looked at it. It was the same one he had encoded earlier for Mr. Willowbrook: MFGW QJ OU NAYYF BT IXV XUC WQFJCIOI DX YNYMN ZX FBADHIGP CHLLPSAOV EI YNLZN.

"I just can't figure it out," Boris said. "I've tried, but it just doesn't make any sense to me."

"Now, Boris," Dinky began, "this message was encoded using Trithemius's Square Table. Remember, it consists of twenty-six alphabets, each one being slid one place to the left of the previous one. Decoding is simply the reverse of encoding. If you'll reverse the steps we used when we encoded your message about missing the boat in New York, then you'll have the contents of this message.''

DINKY WILL DECODE THE SECRET MESSAGE AT THE BEGINNING OF THE NEXT CHAPTER. DO YOU THINK YOU CAN DO IT BEFORE HE DOES?

Chapter Seven

"Here, let me show you," Dinky said. "Let's take the first couple of words in the message: 'MFGW QJ.' Okay, now remember that decoding is the reverse of encoding. 'M' in the secret message would be 'M' in the clear message, because you always start with the first alphabet in Trithemius's Square Table. That's also the clear alphabet. The second letter in the secret message is 'F,' so you find 'F' in the second alphabet, then look *above* it in the first alphabet and you find the letter 'E.' The third letter is 'G.' You find 'G' in the third alphabet, look above it in the first alphabet, and you also find the letter 'E.' If you take each letter in the secret message, find that letter in succeeding alphabets, look *above* it in the first alphabet, then you'll be able to decode the message. The first two words of the secret message, then, are 'MEET ME.' "

"It looks so easy when you do it," Boris said.

Dinky smiled. "The whole message is . . ." He paused for effect. ". . . The whole message is: 'MEET ME IN FRONT OF THE FBI BUILDING AT THREE P.M. TOMORROW. IMPORTANT. BE THERE.' "

Everybody looked expectantly at Boris.

"How clever!" Boris said. "How very clever!"

"What do you mean?" Dinky asked.

"Who would have thought that we'd be dumb enough to have a meeting outside the FBI Building?" Boris said. He laughed. "Leave it to us Bulgarian spies to come up with something this clever!"

"Yeah," Lulu said, "that's really clever."

"Boris," Ethel said, "I know that I shouldn't tell you this, but—"

"Ethel!" Dinky shouted. He gave her a very sharp look.

"Shouldn't tell me what?" Boris said.

"Uh, oh, I, uh, nothing," Ethel stammered.

"Are you really sure you want to go through with this meeting?" Wong asked.

"Yes, yes, I have to," Boris said. "There are a lot of loose ends that I need to tie up."

"And there's nothing that we can do to stop you?" Lulu said.

"No, no," Boris said. "It is my duty. Besides, why would you want to stop me?"

"Uh," Lulu said.

"Uh," Wong said.

"Uh, we're only concerned with your health," Dinky said.

"My health?" Boris looked puzzled.

"Yes," Dinky explained. "We thought that perhaps you might be, uh . . . too tired for this last meeting."

"I jog two miles around the Bulgarian Embassy every day," Boris said. "I am in perfect health."

Ethel began sobbing. "Uh, uh, uhhh!"

Boris put his arms around her shoulders. "Now, now, little cowgirl," he said, "you mustn't do that. Why are you so sad when I am so happy?"

"Because you may never get to see the buffalo roam or the deer and the antelope play, that's why!" Ethel sobbed.

"Dinky! Dinky Lakewood!"

"It's my mother," Dinky said. He stuck his head out the door. "Yes, Mother?"

"It's after seven," Mrs. Lakewood shouted. "Don't you think you'd better quit playing and tell your friends to go home? Tomorrow's another school day, you know."

"Okay, Mother!" Dinky shouted back.

"Playing!" Lulu said indignantly. "Does she actually think we're *playing* in here? Doesn't she realize that decisions affecting the entire world are being made in this . . . this converted toolshed at this very moment? I'll never understand some people. No wonder the world's in such a mess!"

Boris turned to Ethel. "Dear, dear cowgirl," he said, "do not worry about me. I'll have the meeting with my contact tomorrow afternoon at the FBI Building, and then I'll meet you here at six P.M. In the meantime, I want you to buy a couple of tickets on the first bus out for Texas after six o'clock."

"Oh, Boris, do you really mean it?" Ethel said.

Boris looked Ethel straight in the eye. "I mean it," he said.

Ethel squeezed Boris's hand. "You'll make a great ranch foreman," she said. "You'll see."

Boris smiled. "I know," he said. Then he opened the door of the clubhouse and slipped away into the darkness.

Lulu looked at Ethel. "Boy, you really surprise me, you know that?" she said.

"What do you mean?" Ethel said.

"I mean," Lulu said, "crying and carrying on like that! I thought you were . . . well, stronger!"

Ethel blew her nose. "Listen, girlie," she said, "all my life I've had to be the strong one, ever since Daddy ran away in 1920. But I've got feelings, too, you know!"

"Well, it's just that I—" Lulu began.

Ethel stood up. "Well, I guess you'll just have to find somebody else to help you with your code-solving," she interrupted. "Come this time tomorrow night, I'll be on my way to Texas with my ranch foreman."

"Wait a minute, Ethel," Dinky said. "Aren't you forgetting that Boris is walking into a trap?"

Ethel stopped. She began twirling her lasso. "You've never seen me lasso an FBI critter, have you?" she said.

"Now, Ethel," Dinky warned, "you can't interfere with the plans of the FBI. If you do, then you'll destroy the credibility of the Secret Code Service. We'll never ever get any more clients. They'll know we don't keep our word."

"In other words," Wong emphasized, "their secrets won't be our secrets anymore!"

"Right!" said Dinky.

"When it comes to your losing your credibility or my losing my ranch foreman, then you know which one I'm going to choose!" Ethel said. "Blood is thicker than water!"

"Ethel!" Dinky said.

"I knew we should have made her sign a loyalty oath," Lulu said.

"Dinky! Dinky Lakewood!" Mrs. Lakewood shouted from the house. "You come in here right this minute. You need to eat dinner and take a bath!"

"Oh, good grief!" Dinky muttered. "Now listen, Ethel," he said hurriedly. "I can't stay out here all night trying to convince you not to interfere with the FBI."

Ethel put her hands on her hips. "My mind is made up, Mr. Lakewood," she said defiantly. "I shall be at the FBI Building tomorrow at three o'clock to make sure nothing happens to Boris, and that's final!" With that, she stormed out of the clubhouse.

Dinky, Lulu, and Wong could hear the whirring of her lasso far into the night.

"What are we going to do?" Lulu said.

70

"Dinky! Dinky Lakewood!" This time it was *Mr.* Lakewood. "My team is just about to make a touchdown. If I have to come out there and get you and miss that touchdown, I am not going to be very happy about it!"

"Coming, Dad!" Dinky shouted. To Lulu and Wong he said, "Let's decide something quick. School is out at two-fifteen. That's forty-five minutes before Boris's meeting. If we can keep Ethel from causing any trouble, then maybe we can save the Secret Code Service."

"Maybe we can waylay her," Wong said.

"I don't know," Dinky said. "We'll just have to play it by ear. But we have to keep her from interfering until whatever is going to happen has happened."

"Yeah," Wong agreed, "until nature has taken its course."

"Even if it means letting Boris get captured?" Lulu said sadly.

"Lulu," Dinky said softly, "that's a dog-eat-dog world out there. This is just the natural order of things. When we set up this organization, we made an agreement that we would not take sides. We are being tested now. We have to be strong."

"I suppose you have a point, Dinky Lakewood," Lulu said, "a cruel point, but a point nevertheless. Good night!" She put on her beret and dark glasses and left the clubhouse.

"I just remembered," Wong said. "I have to stay after school tomorrow and work on some math problems. See you later."

"Yeah," Dinky said, "see you later." He turned out the light and stood for a moment in the darkness of the clubhouse. A hot shower would feel real good right now, he thought. He only wished it would take his mind off what was about to happen.

*   *   *

"Are you sure this is the right bus?" Lulu asked.

It was 2:20 P.M. Dinky and Lulu had walked the block from their school building and boarded a Number 38 bus. Dinky was clutching a brown paper bag.

"I checked the route map," Dinky said. "This bus stops two blocks from the FBI Building."

"Why didn't we take one that stops right in front?" Lulu demanded. "I've had a hard day!"

"Because I don't want anybody to see us, that's why," Dinky said. "If Ethel sees us, then she'll think we're trying to stop her. There's no telling what she'd do."

"She'd probably try to tie us up with that lasso of hers," Lulu said.

"You're right," Dinky said. "And if either Boris or Mr. Willowbrook sees us, then they'll know that something is wrong and our reputation will be ruined."

The traffic was already getting heavy and the bus was crawling.

"We could have *walked* faster than this," Lulu complained.

Dinky checked his watch. "We'll make it," he said.

Finally, they reached their stop, and Dinky and Lulu got off the bus. Dinky reached into the sack he was carrying.

"What's that?" Lulu asked.

"Glasses with false noses and moustaches," Dinky said. "Put them on. I thought we should wear disguises."

They both put on their glasses.

Lulu stopped and looked at her reflection in a store window. "They'll never recognize us," she said.

Dinky looked in the window, too. "I certainly hope you're right," he said. "But just in case, we still need to be careful. Wait! Look across the street!"

Dinky and Lulu turned around cautiously. Across Pennsylvania Avenue, they could see Ethel. She was dressed in another cowgirl outfit, purple with white fringe, silver sequins, and rhinestones. On her head was a large white hat. She was twirling a lasso.

Dinky and Lulu watched as she turned up Ninth Street, towards E Street and the entrance to the FBI Building.

"Let's follow her," Dinky whispered, "but at a safe distance."

They crossed Pennsylvania and began following Ethel up Ninth Street.

Ethel continued to twirl her lasso as she walked along. She was attracting quite a crowd.

"You know, I don't think she would have made a very good spy after all," Lulu said.

"Why?" Dinky asked.

"She's much too flamboyant," Lulu said.

"Well, right now she's not too interested in becoming a spy," Dinky said. "She's only interested in saving Boris and taking him to Texas so he can be her ranch foreman."

Ethel turned down E Street towards the entrance to the FBI Building. When she reached the entrance, she stopped. Lulu and Dinky ducked behind two parked cars to keep from being seen.

"What's she doing now?" Lulu asked.

Dinky peeked over the hood of the car. "She's just standing there, in front of the entrance," he said, "twirling her lasso."

Lulu looked. "Good grief," she said, "what a spectacle! I can't believe she's so brazen!"

"Well, at least she's entertaining that line of people waiting to take the FBI tour," Dinky admitted.

"Don't look now," Lulu said.

"Where?" Dinky said, looking around.

"I said, don't look!" Lulu whispered.

"Okay, okay, I won't," Dinky said. "But where am I not supposed to look?"

"Across the street," Lulu said. "Do you see those four men standing over there together?"

"How can I see them if I'm not supposed to look?" Dinky asked.

"Oh, all right, go ahead and look," Lulu said. "But be careful."

Dinky looked again. "You mean those four men who're wearing the same kind of glasses with false noses and moustaches that we are?" he said.

"Exactly," Lulu said.

"What about them?" Dinky said.

"Look at the one in the gray suit," Lulu said. "Doesn't he remind you of somebody we know?"

Dinky looked closely. "Hmm," he said, "yes, I . . . of course! It's Mr. Willowbrook. But who are those other men?"

"I bet they're FBI or CIA," Lulu said.

"This whole thing is getting completely out of control," Dinky said.

"I'm sure they're all waiting for Boris," Lulu said. "He . . . wait a minute. I hadn't thought of this until just now. How will they recognize Boris? They've never seen him before!"

"Boris's contact probably told them what to look for," Dinky said. "Remember, Boris told us that all Bulgarian spies receive the same training. They wear the same clothes and walk the same way and everything. I'm sure they'll recognize Boris when they see him."

"Oh, that's right," Lulu said. "Poor Boris."

"Watch the emotions," Dinky said.

"I wonder where he is," Lulu said. "It must be after three o'clock."

Dinky looked at his watch. "It's ten minutes after three," he said. "There's no telling where Boris is."

"All right, you kids! Just what do you think you're doing?"

Dinky and Lulu looked up. A big man smoking a big cigar was standing on the sidewalk looking at them crouched down between the two cars.

"Nothing, sir," Dinky managed to say. "We're just waiting for a friend."

"A likely story," the man said. "I think you're trying to break into my car, that's what I think, and I also think that I'm going to call a policeman." He began looking up and down the street.

"Oh, no, sir," Lulu said hurriedly. "We wouldn't do anything like that. We really are waiting for a friend of ours. He's a Bulgarian spy."

"A *what?*" the man said.

"Nothing," Dinky broke in. "We're just waiting for somebody."

"Well, you can just wait somewhere else," the man said. He pushed his way past them and got into his car.

"Come on," Dinky said to Lulu. "Let's get out of here. That man is definitely capable of violence."

They moved cautiously down the street and hid between two other cars.

Dinky looked at his watch again. "It's already three-thirty," he said, "and still no Boris."

"Can you see what's happening with Ethel?" Lulu asked.

Dinky peeked over the hood of the car. "She's still twirling her lasso," he said. "The people in line are tossing her money."

"How disgusting," Lulu said. "I'm beginning to think that Emma was right about her after all."

Dinky looked across the street. "I don't see Mr. Willowbrook or those other men anymore," he said.

"That's because they just got in line for the FBI tour," Lulu said. She was peeking over the top of the car.

"Uh-oh," Dinky said. "Do you think that Mr. Willowbrook will recognize Ethel?"

"I doubt it," Lulu said. "She's just put on a purple mask that matches her outfit. Besides, even if he does, he'll probably just think that this is the way she earns her living when she's not working for us."

"Well, we'll wait until four o'clock," Dinky said, "and if nothing has happened by then, I think we should go home."

"I think that's a good idea," Lulu said. "I'm getting tired."

By four o'clock nothing had happened, so Lulu and Dinky walked back down to Pennsylvania Avenue and caught a bus home.

"Well, that was a complete waste of time," Lulu said when they were seated at the back of the bus.

"Well, not exactly," Dinky said. "I was beginning to enjoy Ethel's rope tricks. She's really good at that, you know it?"

"She must be," Lulu conceded. "She even had Mr. Willowbrook and those other men tossing coins to her. I bet she made a fortune!"

The bus let them off a block from Dinky's house.

"Well, what do we do now?" Lulu asked.

"I'm not quite sure," Dinky said. "We probably need to go back to the clubhouse and regroup. When we get to my house, I'll call Wong and see if he's finished with his math problems."

"Okay," Lulu said.

When they arrived at the clubhouse, the door was open. They looked inside. In the dim interior, they

76

could make out the figure of a man sitting in one of the chairs.

"Hey, you two, where've you been?" the man asked.

It was Boris.

Chapter Eight

"Boris!" Lulu shouted.

"Boris!" Dinky shouted. "Where were you?"

Boris looked puzzled. "What do you mean, where was I?" he said.

"We thought you were supposed to have a meeting in front of the FBI Building," Lulu said. "We were—"

"Yes, uh," Dinky interrupted, "we were wondering how it went?"

"Well, I *was* supposed to have a meeting," Boris said, "but I got there early, and you know me, I just hate waiting around, doing nothing. There was a line in front of the building, so I asked a man standing in it what it was for. He said it was for the FBI tour. Well, I've always wanted to see the FBI, so I stood in line."

"You took the FBI tour?" Dinky gasped.

"Yes, but I didn't know it would take so long," Boris said. "Of course, part of the reason it took so long was that I got to talking to an FBI agent about all the training he has to go through. You know, those FBI agents are almost as highly trained as I am! Anyway, when I started to leave, I couldn't find my way out of the building, so I just wandered around until the FBI Director finally let me out his private entrance."

"The FBI Director let you out his private entrance?" Lulu gasped.

"Yes," Boris said, "but it was already after four, and I knew that I had missed the meeting with my contact, so I just decided to come on back here. I guess I'll have to leave another message for him."

"You're amazing, Boris," Lulu said, "simply amazing."

Boris smiled. "Yes, I guess I am," he said.

Wong opened the door to the clubhouse and came in. "Sorry, I'm late," he said, "but those math problems were harder than I had expected." He looked at Boris. "How'd the meeting go?"

"It's a long story," Boris said.

"Are you going to try and have another meeting with your contact?" Dinky asked.

"No," Boris said, "but I do want to leave him a message. I hate to run off without saying good-bye. Will you encode it for me?"

"Sure," Dinky said, "what's the message?"

"Sorry I missed you. FBI tour was great. Am going to Texas. Say hello to everybody in Sofia for me," Boris said.

"Shall we encode this one using Trithemius's Square Table, too?" Dinky asked.

"No, I think it would be a good idea if we used a different code," Boris said. "I know that I'm not supposed to do that, but . . . well, since this is my last message, I'd really like to impress the people back in Sofia. Here's my codebook. Let's come up with something really clever this time."

Dinky took the copy of *All the Bulgarian Codes You'll Ever Need!* and began thumbing through the pages.

"Won't you get into trouble for deserting?" Wong asked. "Don't they shoot spies who do that?"

"No, we're a pretty easygoing bunch," Boris said. "They'll probably just be a little put out, that's all."

"I'm disillusioned," Lulu said.

Boris looked at Dinky. "Found a good one yet?" he asked.

"The Beaufort Square looks good," Dinky said. "I think we'll use that."

"Whatever you say," Boris said. "I have complete faith in you."

"The Beaufort Square consists of twenty-seven alphabets," Dinky explained, "the first and last letters of each alphabet being repetitions. Each alphabet shifts one space to the left of the previous one." Dinky began writing:

```
A B C D E F G H I J K L M N O P Q R S T U V W X Y Z A
B C D E F G H I J K L M N O P Q R S T U V W X Y Z A B
C D E F G H I J K L M N O P Q R S T U V W X Y Z A B C
D E F G H I J K L M N O P Q R S T U V W X Y Z A B C D
E F G H I J K L M N O P Q R S T U V W X Y Z A B C D E
F G H I J K L M N O P Q R S T U V W X Y Z A B C D E F
G H I J K L M N O P Q R S T U V W X Y Z A B C D E F G
H I J K L M N O P Q R S T U V W X Y Z A B C D E F G H
I J K L M N O P Q R S T U V W X Y Z A B C D E F G H I
J K L M N O P Q R S T U V W X Y Z A B C D E F G H I J
K L M N O P Q R S T U V W X Y Z A B C D E F G H I J K
L M N O P Q R S T U V W X Y Z A B C D E F G H I J K L
M N O P Q R S T U V W X Y Z A B C D E F G H I J K L M
N O P Q R S T U V W X Y Z A B C D E F G H I J K L M N
O P Q R S T U V W X Y Z A B C D E F G H I J K L M N O
P Q R S T U V W X Y Z A B C D E F G H I J K L M N O P
Q R S T U V W X Y Z A B C D E F G H I J K L M N O P Q
R S T U V W X Y Z A B C D E F G H I J K L M N O P Q R
S T U V W X Y Z A B C D E F G H I J K L M N O P Q R S
T U V W X Y Z A B C D E F G H I J K L M N O P Q R S T
U V W X Y Z A B C D E F G H I J K L M N O P Q R S T U
V W X Y Z A B C D E F G H I J K L M N O P Q R S T U V
W X Y Z A B C D E F G H I J K L M N O P Q R S T U V W
X Y Z A B C D E F G H I J K L M N O P Q R S T U V W X
Y Z A B C D E F G H I J K L M N O P Q R S T U V W X Y
Z A B C D E F G H I J K L M N O P Q R S T U V W X Y Z
A B C D E F G H I J K L M N O P Q R S T U V W X Y Z A
```

"That looks interesting," Boris said.

Lulu and Wong looked. "I don't think I'm familiar with that one," Lulu said.

"Now, then," Dinky continued, "with the Beaufort Square, you have to choose what is called a *Key Letter* in order to encode a message."

"Hmm," Boris said, "I've always liked the letter 'H.' "

"Then we'll use 'H' as our Key Letter," Dinky said. "Now, the message you want encoded is: 'SORRY I MISSED YOU. FBI TOUR WAS GREAT. AM GOING TO TEXAS. SAY HELLO TO EVERYBODY IN SOFIA FOR ME.' Is that correct?"

"That's correct," Boris said.

"All right," Dinky said, "we'll begin with the word 'SORRY.' First of all, find 'S' in the top alphabet. Go down the column until you reach the letter 'H,' which is our Key Letter. Then turn at a right angle to come out at the side of the square and you'll see the letter 'P.' So in this code, with the Key Letter 'H,' 'S' equals 'P.' Now, the second letter in 'SORRY' is 'O,' so let's find 'O' in the top alphabet, go down the column until we reach the letter 'H,' turn at a right angle to come out at the side of the square, and what do we have?"

" 'T'!" Lulu shouted proudly.

Dinky gave her an exasperated look. "Correct," he said. "And if we continue encoding the rest of the word 'SORRY,' we'll see that 'R' equals 'Q' twice, and 'Y' equals 'J.' The word 'SORRY' would then be encoded as 'PTQQJ.' "

"I think I'm actually beginning to understand this," Boris said. "If you'd been my teacher at the Sofia Spy School, then maybe I wouldn't have had so much trouble."

Dinky beamed.

"If I ever hear of an opening there, I'll let you

know," Boris said. "Now, why don't you let me try to do the second word?"

"Okay," Dinky said, "what would the word 'I' be?"

"Let me see," Boris said. He found 'I' in the top alphabet, went down the column until he reached the Key Letter 'H,' then turned at a right angle until he came to the end of the square. " 'Z'!" he said triumphantly. " 'I' equals 'Z'!"

"Correct," Dinky said. "So 'SORRY I' would be encoded as 'PTQQJ Z.' Do you want to do the rest of the message?"

"I don't know," Boris said with a sigh. "That was quite a strain on me, just doing that one word. If you don't mind—"

"I don't mind," Dinky said. He began to encode the rest of the message. When he finished, he had: PTQQJ Z VZPPDE JTN CGZ OTNQ LHP BQDHO HV BTZUB OT ODKHP PHJ ADWWT OT DMDQJGTEJ ZU PTXZH CTQ VD.

"Now, I need to take this message to . . . let's see, what day is this?" Boris hesitated.

"This is Tuesday," Lulu said.

"Oh, that's right, Tuesday," Boris said. "That means that today's drop is in Lafayette Park." He looked at his watch. "If I hurry, I can run home, change clothes, pack, get this message in the drop before my contact makes his rounds, and still make it to the bus station on time."

"Be careful, Boris," Lulu said.

"Yeah," Wong added, "take care of yourself."

"Boris . . ." Dinky started to say. But the motto of the Secret Code Service flashed before his eyes: *Your Secrets Are Our Secrets!* What a struggle, he thought. ". . . Oh, nothing," he said.

"Don't worry about me," Boris said. "You guys keep forgetting that I am a highly trained Bulgarian spy.

I know what I'm doing." He stumbled over a chair as he started out the door of the clubhouse. Dinky, Lulu, and Wong helped him to his feet. Boris brushed himself off. "Oh, I just remembered something," he said. "I told Ethel that I would meet her *here*. What am I going to do?"

"Don't worry," Dinky said. "We'll tell Ethel that you'll meet her at the bus station just as soon after six o'clock as you can."

Tears came to Boris's eyes. "Boy, you people are just super," he said. Then he left the clubhouse.

Dinky, Lulu, and Wong watched as Boris opened the back gate and disappeared down the alley.

"Do you think they'll get him this time?" Lulu asked.

"Who knows?" Dinky said.

"Dinky, your soup is ready!" Mrs. Lakewood shouted from the house. "Come on in and eat!"

"Okay, Mom!" Dinky shouted back. To Lulu and Wong, he said, "Would you two like a bowl of hot soup?"

"That sounds good," Lulu said, "but do you think we could eat it out here? Things are beginning to get pretty busy around this place and we can't take a chance on missing out on anything."

"She's right," Wong said.

"That's a good idea," Dinky agreed. "I'll have it sent out here."

When Dinky returned with a tray with three bowls of hot soup and some crackers, Ethel was sitting in the clubhouse. She was crying. "I was too late," she sobbed.

Dinky put down the tray. "Too late for what?" he asked.

Ethel picked up a bowl of soup. "Thanks so much," she sniffed. "I'm awfully hungry."

Lulu and Wong picked up the other two bowls.

Dinky looked at the empty tray, sighed, then repeated, "Too late for what, Ethel?"

"Boris must have been arrested," Ethel said. She sipped a spoonful of soup. "I waited and waited and waited in front of the FBI Building and he never showed up. I even earned enough money while I was waiting to buy the biggest ranch in Texas!"

"How'd you do that?" Wong asked.

"It's a long story," Lulu said.

"Oh, I'll never see him again," Ethel sobbed. "And he would have made such a good foreman for my ranch!"

"I've been trying to tell her," Lulu said to Dinky, "but she hasn't given me the chance."

Ethel looked up through bloodshot eyes. "Tell me what?" she said.

"Boris is all right," Dinky said.

"All . . . uhuh, uhuh . . . right? Are . . . uhuh, uhuh . . . you . . . uhuh, uhuh . . . sure?" Ethel managed to say.

"He was just here a few minutes ago," Wong said.

"He's on his way to Lafayette Park to deliver his last message," Lulu said. "He wants you to meet him at the bus station instead of here."

"He'll be there just as soon after six o'clock as he can," Dinky added.

Ethel's voice steadied. "Well, what time is it now?" she asked.

Dinky looked at his watch. "It's six-fifteen," he said.

"Good heavens!" Ethel said. "The bus to Texas leaves at seven!" She stood up. Two rhinestones and several sequins fell from her dress. "I have to pack. I can't wait around here!" She hesitated.

"What's wrong?" Lulu asked.

"I'm just wondering if Momma and Emma will give me any trouble for running off like this," Ethel said.

"You're of age," Dinky said, "surely—"

"That doesn't matter to Momma," Ethel said. "She has friends in high places." She looked at Dinky. "But I hate to go without leaving them a message." She thought for a minute. "What about: *Gone to Texas. Will write from the ranch.* Could you put that in code so I could leave it with them? Nothing too hard or Emma will never figure it out."

"We could use a simple reverse code," Dinky said. "That's where you start with the last word and reverse the letters of the entire message."

"That sounds good," Ethel said. "I think Emma could figure that out eventually. She's usually just a few days behind on those word puzzles in the newspaper."

"Okay," Dinky said, "if we take 'GONE TO TEXAS. WILL WRITE FROM THE RANCH' and simply reverse it, we'll have 'HCNAR EHT MORF ETIRW LLIW SAXET OT ENOG.' "

Ethel looked at the message. "Well, that may take Emma longer than I thought," she said, "but it's good enough. How much do I owe you?"

"It's on the house," Dinky said.

Lulu looked perturbed.

"Then, put 'er there, partner!" Ethel said. She held out her hand and Dinky shook it.

"Be sure and write," Dinky said.

"We'll be interested in hearing what kind of ranch foreman Boris makes," Wong said.

"I'll do that," Ethel said, "but I wouldn't worry about Boris."

"Somebody needs to worry about him," Lulu muttered.

After Ethel had gone, Dinky said, "I think she barely touched that soup. I think I'll eat the rest of it."

"Well," Lulu said, "I guess it's all over."

"What's all over?" Dinky said. He took a sip of soup.

"Our work in the Secret Code Service," Lulu said.

"It most certainly is not!" Dinky exclaimed. "This is just our first case. And I'm not even sure that this one is over yet. And I won't be sure until we hear from Boris and Ethel that they've arrived in Texas and have settled in at the ranch. Besides, I'm quite sure that we're going to have another—"

"Oh, Mr. Lakewood! Are you in there?"

"—Visitor just any time now," Dinky continued.

Dinky, Lulu, and Wong looked up. In the darkness outside the clubhouse door, they could make out the outline of Mr. Willowbrook. This time he wasn't alone. There were three other men with him. Lulu and Dinky recognized them as the three men they had seen earlier across from the FBI Building. They all still had on the glasses with the false noses and moustaches.

"Come in," Dinky said.

Mr. Willowbrook came inside, followed by the other three men. "I'd like for you to meet Inspector Longbeach from the FBI," Mr. Willowbrook said, "and Mr. Inglewood from the CIA, and General Pico Rivera from Military Intelligence."

Everybody shook hands.

"Sit down, gentlemen," Dinky said. Lulu and Wong remained standing. "Now, what may we do for you?"

"I'm afraid we have bad news for you," Mr. Willowbrook said.

Dinky, Lulu, and Wong tensed.

"What's wrong?" Dinky finally asked.

"We didn't capture Boris the Bad Bulgarian after all," Mr. Willowbrook said with a sigh.

Dinky, Lulu, and Wong relaxed.

"But there is some good news, too," General Pico Rivera announced.

"What's the good news?" Lulu asked.

"We did find another message that he left," Mr. Willowbrook said. "In Lafayette Park."

"Say, how did *you* know which park he was going to use?" Wong asked. All four men turned towards him. Wong felt himself shrinking.

"We didn't," Mr. Willowbrook explained. "We have men covering all the parks."

"Yeah, we thought we had him once," Inspector Longbeach said. "There was this guy acting awfully suspicious."

"But he was dressed in a cowboy outfit," Mr. Inglewood added.

Dinky, Lulu, and Wong looked at each other.

"And our intelligence tells us that Bulgarian spies never wear cowboy clothes," Mr. Willowbrook said.

General Pico Rivera handed the message to Dinky. "Do you think you can decode this?" he said.

Dinky looked at his watch. "My watch has stopped," he said. "What time is it?"

"It's almost seven o'clock," Mr. Willowbrook said.

"Good," Lulu said, "the bus leaves at seven."

"What bus?" Inspector Longbeach asked.

Lulu looked at him. "The seven o'clock bus, of course!" she said. "The seven o'clock bus always leaves at seven!"

"I wouldn't be too sure about that," Wong said. "I remember once when the seven o'clock bus left after seven. In fact, it wasn't too long ago."

"That must have been when they were on strike," Dinky said. "I don't think they're on strike now."

"I don't think so, either," Lulu said.

"Wait a minute! Wait a minute!" Mr. Willowbrook said. "Who cares when the seven o'clock bus leaves? What difference does it make?"

"Well, if you were planning to catch the seven o'clock bus, it would make a lot of difference," Lulu said.

"Well, I'm not," Mr. Willowbrook said. "Besides, this message is more important than catching any seven o'clock bus!" He looked at Dinky. "Can you or can you not decode it?"

"What time is it *now?*" Dinky asked.

"Oh, good grief," Mr. Inglewood said. He looked at his watch. "It's five minutes after seven."

"Good," Dinky said. "Yes, I can decode this message."

The four men looked at each other.

Dinky looked at the message. It was the same one he had encoded earlier for Boris. He closed his eyes. He had an image of Boris and Ethel on the bus, headed for Texas. "Yes, I feel it coming," he whispered. "This is the Beaufort Square and the message is . . . any minute now . . ."

"This guy's great, isn't he?" Mr. Willowbrook said.

"The CIA needs him," Mr. Inglewood said.

"No, no," Inspector Longbeach said. "The FBI needs him more."

"Gentlemen, gentlemen," General Pico Rivera said, "the military could use him to better advantage."

"I've got it!" Dinky shouted.

"What does it say?" all four men asked in unison.

"It says . . ." Dinky paused for effect. ". . . It says: 'SORRY I MISSED YOU. FBI TOUR WAS GREAT. AM GOING TO TEXAS. SAY HELLO TO EVERY-BODY IN SOFIA FOR ME.' "

The four men looked stunned. Inspector Longbeach finally said, "You mean he was actually inside the FBI Building and we didn't capture him?"

"What cunning, what gall," Mr. Inglewood said. "We need somebody like that on our side!"

"We'll never capture him if he goes to Texas," General Pico Rivera said.

"Why not?" Lulu asked.

"We just don't have the men and equipment to look under every tumbleweed and cactus," General Pico Rivera explained. "That could tie up the whole Army!"

"Listen to yourselves, gentlemen," Mr. Willowbrook said sarcastically. "Just listen to yourselves!"

The three men flushed with embarrassment.

"What were we saying?" Mr. Inglewood asked.

"You were saying that you actually believed the contents of this message," Mr. Willowbrook said.

"*You* don't?" Inspector Longbeach said.

"Of course not," Mr. Willowbrook said proudly. "If you'd been in the business as long as I have, then you'd know that this is all a trick to throw us off his track."

"He's putting us on?" Inspector Longbeach said.

"He's kidding us?" Mr. Inglewood said.

"This is all a joke?" General Pico Rivera said.

"Of course it is," Mr. Willowbrook said. "This man is cunning. This man is brilliant. This man is dangerous. And this man is still in Washington!"

"What time is it?" Lulu asked.

"It's seven-thirty," Mr. Willowbrook said. "And I think you people need to get a clock for this place."

"Are you sure about that?" Inspector Longbeach said.

"Of course I'm sure," Mr. Willowbrook said. "My watch is never wrong."

"No, no, no," Inspector Longbeach said, "I mean, that this Boris fellow is still in Washington?"

"Oh, yes, yes, yes," Mr. Willowbrook said, "yes, I am! Boris the Bad Bulgarian is still in Washington, and he's laughing at us right this minute. He thinks we're on our way to Texas. But the last laugh will be on him."

"But where in Washington is he?" Mr. Inglewood asked.

"Don't you see, gentlemen?" Mr. Willowbrook said.

"I'm afraid not," Inspector Longbeach said.

"Me, either," General Pico Rivera said.

"He's taunting us," Mr. Willowbrook explained. "He's teasing us. He's gone to ground in a new safe house on . . . *Texas Avenue!*"

"Brilliant!" the three men echoed.

Mr. Willowbrook looked at Dinky. "I want to send another message to this Boris," he said. "We'll leave copies of it in parks all over the District of Columbia. Sooner or later, he won't be able to resist seeing if we have left a message for him. Then we'll make our move!"

Dinky raised his eyebrow at Lulu and Wong. "Well, you're paying for it," he said. "What's the message?"

Mr. Willowbrook got out a piece of paper and a pen and hurriedly wrote out the message. Then he handed it to Dinky. "Use the same code as last time," he said.

Dinky read the message: "*Sit in car outside safe house on Texas Avenue. Wait for contact.* Okay," he said, "I'll encode this using the Beaufort Square and the Key Letter 'H.' "

DINKY WILL ENCODE THIS MESSAGE IN THE NEXT CHAPTER, USING THE BEAUFORT SQUARE AND THE KEY LETTER 'H.' CAN YOU DO IT BEFORE HE DOES?

Chapter Nine

"Here's the message," Dinky said. He handed it to Mr. Willowbrook.

Mr. Willowbrook looked at it: PZO ZU FHQ TNOPZ-ED PHCDATNPD TU ODKHP HMDUND LHZO CTQ FTUOHFO. "Thanks, Mr. Lakewood," he said. "Your country owes you a debt of gratitude."

Lulu sighed. "And ten dollars, as well," she added.

"Oh, yes, well, I seem to be short of change." Mr. Willowbrook turned towards the other three men. "Gentlemen?" he said.

Mr. Inglewood took out his wallet. "Let me see, now," he said. "I have one . . . two . . . three . . . four . . . five . . . six . . . seven . . . eight . . . nine . . . ten . . . ten one-dollar bills here, but uh-oh, I forgot. I have to pick up a loaf of bread and some milk on the way home. I guess I could chip in five dollars, though." He handed the five dollars to Dinky.

"That still leaves five dollars," Lulu said. "What about the rest of you guys?"

"How about you, General Pico Rivera?" Mr. Willowbrook said.

"I only carry credit cards," General Pico Rivera said. He looked at Dinky. "Do you take American Express?"

"Not yet," Dinky said, "but that's a good idea!"

"Inspector Longbeach?" Mr. Willowbrook said.

"I'm under orders to cut down on my expense account," Inspector Longbeach said, "but I suppose I could let you have three dollars, too."

"We're still short two dollars," Lulu persisted.

"We can't run a business if our clients don't pay, gentlemen," Wong added.

Mr. Willowbrook sighed. "Well, let me look in my wallet," he said. "I do keep some money tucked away for emergencies." He took out two dollars. "I was saving this for . . . but never mind!" He handed it to Dinky.

"Thanks," Lulu said.

"I'd like a receipt, please," Mr. Willowbrook said.

"Our receipt books are still at the printer's," Lulu said. "I haven't forgotten. I'll mail them to you."

"Well, all right," Mr. Willowbrook said. "Come on, men, we need to start putting this message in all the parks in the District of Columbia! At once!"

After the men had left, Dinky, Lulu, and Wong sat down.

"Boy, what a day!" Lulu said.

"Yeah," Wong agreed.

Dinky looked around the clubhouse. "This place is a mess," he said. "Let's straighten it up and then call it a night."

Two hours later, the clubhouse was in order.

"You know, Dinky Lakewood," Lulu said, "it occurred to me last night that you're the only one who's been encoding and decoding secret messages around here. I somehow feel . . . well, somewhat . . . how shall I put it . . . unfulfilled!"

"It really wasn't planned, Lulu," Dinky said. "It just

seemed to work out that way, that's all. I'm sorry if it bothers you.''

Lulu arched an eyebrow and tilted her head. "Well, we *will* do something about it, won't we?" she said.

Dinky swallowed hard. "Certainly, Lulu," he said.

"Do you think that Mr. Willowbrook will ever catch Boris?" Wong asked.

"I doubt it," Dinky said, happy that Wong had changed the subject. "He doesn't believe that he went to Texas."

"What do you think he'll do?" Lulu asked.

"Well, he'll probably keep putting messages in all the parks in Washington until he realizes that nobody has picked them up and then I suppose he'll just assume that Boris went back to Bulgaria," Dinky said.

There was a sudden noise outside the clubhouse door.

"What was that?" Lulu said. She grabbed for her beret and dark glasses.

"Oh, I certainly hope that Boris didn't miss that bus," Wong said.

"That would be disastrous," Dinky said.

The door to the clubhouse opened slowly. A tall, skinny woman stuck her head inside. "Is this the headquarters of the Secret Code Service?" she asked.

"Yes, it is," Dinky said.

"I'm looking for a Mr. Dinky Lakewood," the woman said.

"I'm Dinky Lakewood," Dinky said.

"You're *Mr.* Lakewood?" the woman asked.

"That's right," Dinky said.

"Well, actually, I was expecting someone . . ." The woman hesitated. She looked from Dinky to Lulu to Wong. "Who are you people, anyway, the *Codebreaker Kids?*" She laughed heartily.

Lulu stiffened. "This is a very serious business operation!" she declared.

"Oh, I'm sorry," the woman said hurriedly, "I really didn't mean—"

"Actually, that's kind of catchy," Dinky said. "The Codebreaker Kids!"

"Yeah," Wong agreed, "it is!"

Lulu looked disgusted.

"What may we do for you?" Dinky asked.

The woman came inside and sat down. "My name's Annie," she said, "and I'm from Albania. I'm also a spy!"

"We cater to spies," Lulu said. She arched an eyebrow and looked at the woman. "*Serious* spies," she added. "What was it you wanted?"

"Well, I'm kind of new at this," Annie explained. "I just arrived yesterday. I was told that my contact would leave a message for me at our drop in Rock Creek Park. I waited around all day today and finally, just a few minutes ago, I saw these four funny-looking men leave a piece of paper in a hollow tree. I thought it was meant for me."

"What did these men look like?" Dinky asked.

"They had on glasses with false noses and moustaches," Annie said.

Dinky, Lulu, and Wong looked at each other.

"Please go on," Lulu said.

"Well, anyway," Annie continued, "as I said, I thought the message was for me, so I took it out of the tree. I tried to decode it on the bus on the way back to my hotel room. But I couldn't! I've been through all the codes in *All the Albanian Codes You'll Ever Need!* but I can't find anything that makes sense."

"How did you find out about us?" Wong asked.

"That's the funny thing," Annie replied. "It must have been fate. While I was on that bus, I found a piece of paper advertising your services. It was stuck behind

94

the seat. So I came on over here. Do you think that you can help me?"

"Let me see the message," Dinky said. Annie handed him the piece of paper. Dinky looked at it for a moment. "Yes, I'm sure we'll be able to help you," he said. He handed the piece of paper to Lulu. "She's all yours," he added.

Chapter Ten

Two weeks after Boris and Ethel went to Texas,
letters began arriving at the Secret Code Service. They
were all written in code. Do you think you can decode
them?

If you have trouble, the solutions follow each letter.

LETTER NO. 1

LOOQ JVLYY
KJCWYAOCAV VOJYR
ACAJIK JYFCK

ZYCL ZUPSE RIRI CPZ GOPW

YJVYR TO CPP CPZ U CLLUHYZ KCXYRE UP
JYFCK GVOK TO CPP EOI CKS KVYK JVY AUC
CWYPJ U QYJ OP JVY BIK GYLY NRCPPUPW JO
WYJ QCLLUYZ YJVYR GURR BY JVY QCUZ OX
VOPOL ZUPSE ZO EOI JVUPS EOI AOIRZ BY QE
BYKJ QCP

EOIL XLUYPZ
BOLUK BIRWCL

(Hint: Use the Beaufort Square with the Key Letter 'C.')

97

SOLUTION TO LETTER NO. 1

Room Three
Stagecoach Hotel
Cactus, Texas

Dear Dinky, Lulu, and Wong,

Ethel, Jo Ann, and I arrived safely in Texas. Who's Jo Ann you ask? She's the CIA agent I met on the bus. We're planning to get married. Ethel will be the Maid of Honor. Dinky, do you think you could be my best man?

Your friend,
Boris Bulgar

LETTER NO. 2

RGYIJA OUGACPICJ PCJDK
ML OLX RLUP
DCDTUQ TBXCQ

EBCP EIJFY GUGU CJE WLJA

BTKBG RIJCGGY RLUJE C PCJDK QKB WCJTBE
TL OUY QKBQ TBCDKIJA SL CJJ CJE HB KLW TL
PIEB KLPQBQ CJE PLMB QTBBPQ BTKBG QCYQ
IH CGPBCEY C ALLE PCJDK RLPBHCJ SL CJJ CJE
I CPB ALIJA TL KBGM KBP OUIGE C JBW PCJDK
KLUQB

YLUP RPIBJE
OLPIQ OUGACP

MQ QLPPY YLU DLUGEJT HCFB IT TL TKB
WBEEIJA

(Hint: Use the Key Words 'Codebreaker Kids.')

99

SOLUTION TO LETTER NO. 2

Flying Bulgarian Ranch
P.O. Box Four
Cactus, Texas

Dear Dinky, Lulu, and Wong,

Ethel finally found a ranch she wanted to buy. She's teaching Jo Ann and me how to ride horses and rope steers. Ethel says I'm already a good ranch foreman. Jo Ann and I are going to help her build a new ranch house.

Your friend,
Boris Bulgar

P.S. Sorry you couldn't make it to the wedding.

LETTER NO. 3

MSFPUN IBSNHYPHU YHUJO
WV IVE MVBY
JHJABZ ALEHZ

KLHY KPURF SBSB HUK DVUN

DL IBPSA AOL ULD YHUJO OVBZL VU AVW VM
H YHAASLZUHRL KLU DLYL SPCPUN PU H IPN
ALUA BUAPS DL JHU NLA PA TVCLK QV HUUZ
MYPLUK MYVT AOL ZAHAL KLWHYATLUA
JHTL VBA MYVT DHZOPUNAVU MVY H CPZPA
OL ZHPK AOHA AOLYL DHZ ZVTLAOPUN HIVBA
TL AOHA DHZ MHTPSPHY OPZ UHTL PZ
DPSSVDIYVVR

FVBY MYPLUK
IVYPZ IBSNHY

(Hint: Run down the alphabet.)

101

SOLUTION TO LETTER NO. 3

Flying Bulgarian Ranch
P.O. Box Four
Cactus, Texas

Dear Dinky, Lulu, and Wong,

We built the new ranch house on top of a rattlesnake den. We're living in a big tent until we can get it moved. Jo Ann's friend from the State Department came out from Washington for a visit. He said that there was something about me that was familiar. His name is Willowbrook.

Your friend,
Boris Bulgar

LETTER NO. 4

FMALRL HBTPKCUNB GQEUA
JJ XLV EOVT
FEHZBA COIMF

RTQI VBHFU ISKU BPG ATTN

QV DLWVBV ZF SGH OK PMEIB VR QJKA UH
PLYVZN IYW AIKAP RN DP URQJ CVZT PZD GVT
SZS PBDHB QGET VKIWK PTU CPZQ MDK R
HHMO YXPC FSQP FZRNIASL

KBIG VIAXHY
XLPHS CWOKFX

WA NDSQY SAEGWW SZOQCQDBA ZMYN APN
QZHRFCEI GY NZTXQ

(Hint: One of the codes Dinky used will decode this
letter. It's up to you to find the right one!)

SOLUTION TO LETTER NO. 4

Flying Bulgarian Ranch
P.O. Box Four
Cactus, Texas

Dear Dinky, Lulu, and Wong,

I'm taking Jo Ann to Sofia to meet my family. She hopes to do some work for the CIA while she's there. I'll send you a post card from Bulgaria.

Your friend,
Boris Bulgar

P.S. Ethel eloped yesterday with the Governor of Texas!

(Hint: Use Trithemius's Square Table.)